Bright Clouds

HAO JAN

FOREIGN LANGUAGES PRESS
PEKING 1974

ILLUSTRATIONS BY
TUNG CHEN-SHENG
CHEN YU-HSIEN

Printed in the People's Republic of China

Contents

Contents

The Lean Chestnut Horse

HARVEST time. Once again I was on my way to the "East Is Red" Agricultural Co-operative.

Autumn fields were a vast sea of golden waves.

About noon the bus took me to Yangchen Town. I alighted. Carrying my bedding roll on my back, I walked through the noisy waiting room and headed straight for the inn with stables for mules and horses. Here, on the days when country fairs were held, the transport team of the agricultural co-op often stopped for a rest, and it would be convenient for me to get a lift on their cart.

The innkeeper was quick to recognize me. "Comrade Liang," he greeted me smiling, "you've come just in time. Chiao Kuei's come with his cart again. He has un-harnessed the animal and gone to the livestock fair. He'll be back in a few minutes."

I was pleased with this information. I took a stool and sat down by the window to wait for Chiao Kuei and watch the passers-by. Chiao Kuei's image appeared in my mind every time I saw a horse cart. For the last six months I had been impressed by his good deeds, and also worried for him.

Chiao Kuei was a member of the co-op's transport team. He was in his mid twenties, of small stature and with a round face. An excellent driver, he could manage and tame any spirited horse or mule and make it take his orders. You could feel safe riding on his cart.

It was in this town that I had first got acquainted with Chiao Kuei. That afternoon I had failed to hire a cart and was wandering in the street not knowing what to do when I chanced to meet Kuei Jung, a woman volunteer teacher in the "East Is Red" Co-op. I went up to her and said, "I'm going to your co-op, but I can't find a cart. I'm stuck here."

"That's easy to arrange," said she. "Two carts have come from the co-op and they'll go back empty this afternoon. Let's go to the fair now. They're selling a horse there."

So I was saved! Relieved of anxiety I deposited my bedding roll at the inn and went out with Kuei Jung to look for the transport man.

It was a great day at the fair. The streets were so crowded and noisy that two people face to face could not hear each other's voice.

As we were walking we saw a tall slender young man emerging from the crowd and striding towards us. He had a long whip in his right hand, while his left was in the pocket of his black cotton-padded coat. He looked sullen.

"Brother Fu-shun," the woman teacher asked, "have you sold the horse? How much did you get for it?"

The young fellow scowled. "Sold it? Why, we had already settled the price when that model peasant said we couldn't sell it!"

"Why did he stop you?" Kuei Jung wanted to know. "Didn't the co-op decide to give you 300 yuan to buy a new horse once the old one was sold?"

Pointing in the direction of the fair, Fu-shun said, "Go and ask him. Isn't that him coming now?"

I turned to look and saw a young man leading a lean chestnut out of the market. The man's face was tanned, with two dark eyebrows drawn into knots. His head drooping, he held the tether in both hands behind his back as he walked in slow steps.

Kuei Jung went up to him and said almost reproachfully, "Chiao Kuei, why did you stop the sale when the price had been settled? Hadn't the leadership made the decision?"

The transport man was irritated. "I won't have it," said he. "They offer only 30 yuan and they'll take the chestnut to the slaughter house. I've told Fu-shun that I'll give him my brown mule in exchange for the chestnut."

As if pricked by a needle Kuei Jung cried, "Are you crazy? Why do you want to swap your good animal for a bad one? Aren't you going to work any more?"

"It's the same, good or bad," was the reply.

As I could not join their conversation I walked over to the chestnut to examine it. No wonder Fu-shun wanted to sell it. It was really in bad shape. The hair on its front and back parts was all off, its body coated with mud. A mere skeleton in loose skin, a strong wind would have blown it down. Was it worth keeping?

Chiao Kuei watched me looking his horse over. Afraid I might comment, he pointed to the animal and said, "Don't judge it by its looks. It won't die yet. It wasn't

3

like this half a year ago, but because someone wanted to sell it and buy a new one it has been neglected. Who is responsible for this?"

These words were obviously meant for Fu-shun, whose face immediately reddened. He strode towards the inn swinging his whip in anger. A few minutes later, he led over the brown mule which he had just exchanged and purposely passed Chiao Kuei. The transport man did not even give him a glance but went to harness the horse. Fu-shun swung his whip, blinked and said seriously, "I say, Chiao Kuei, I really haven't the heart to use your good animal. Better sell that lean chestnut. What do you say?"

Chiao Kuei did not even look up as he said, "Don't talk nonsense. Let's go."

We reached the village at dusk. People who had heard that Chiao Kuei and others were returning from the fair with a new animal crowded round the carts.

Transport team leader Li Yung squeezed himself into the crowd and shouted to Fu-shun, "You've taken the old animal back! What's the matter with you!"

Before Fu-shun could answer, Chiao Kuei walked up to Li Yung and said calmly, "The lean chestnut was not sold, so no new animal was bought. Here is the 300 yuan to be returned to the co-op."

The team leader looked disappointed and, as he walked away, said, "Let Fu-shun keep the money. Since you didn't sell the horse this time you'll have to sell it at the next fair for any price you can get. You'll need the money to buy a good animal."

"No. There'll be no selling at the next fair, and no buying either."

4

"Why wasn't it sold? Was it because nobody wanted that animal, or because you couldn't buy a new one?"

"Someone wanted it but offered only 30 yuan and I refused to sell it. Instead, I gave Fu-shun my brown mule in exchange for the chestnut."

"What! Why did you refuse? Do you like that lean animal, or are you just stupid?" The team leader's words were sharp enough, though not hasty or heavy.

"That horse can still work. I can't let a useful animal go to the slaughter house. I can't let co-op property drain away. I have a reason for what I've done. . . ."

While Chiao Kuei calmly explained himself, Li Yung's irritation was mounting. He jumped to his feet and cried, "You can't do things any way you like. You have to go by the decision. Ours is a collective organization handling our affairs in a big way. To be mean and stingy is disgusting!"

Chiao Kuei was not swayed. He said confidently, "I wouldn't show off with public money. If you shy off from reason so, why don't you sell all your draught animals and buy motor trucks? Then you'll have your *big* way!" And with that he strode off with his horse.

A new moon came up, bathing the village in silver. I had finished my discussions on work with the co-op cadres when its chairman, Hsiao Yung-shun, said he would take me to Chiao's home to stay. Chiao Kuei was a bachelor, and his mother was away visiting relatives. I was pleased with the arrangement. While we walked along I told Hsiao what I knew about the chestnut horse. He thought for a while and said, "Chiao Kuei is a fine co-op member. Last year he attended the county conference of model workers and peasants. His thinking and way of doing things are significant, remarkable. . . ."

We had crossed the Golden Hen Creek and turned north when suddenly we saw a man walking slowly through the poplars, leading an animal. The co-op chairman recognized him and called, "Chiao Kuei! Hey there!"

But Chiao Kuei did not hear. At that same moment Fu-shun caught up with us. Smiling smugly at another's misfortune, he said, "All the animals in our team are in good shape, except his. When the contest is held, all of us will put on a good show. No one will take responsibility for what happens to that lame mare of his!"

"Fu-shun," said Hsiao Yung-shun, "I'm not criticizing you. You're all right on many things. You just can't think for yourself. Someone draws a line, you take it as a river. Someone says something is good, you rush for it. But you don't know why you do it. Would you ever sell a big horse of your own for 30 yuan? Chiao Kuei is right, but instead of supporting him you make irresponsible and carping comments from the side lines. You are wrong!"

When Hsiao saw Fu-shun lowering his gaze, speechless, he added, "Now take Comrade Liang and walk slowly while I catch up with Chiao Kuei."

Fu-shun was embarrassed at receiving criticism, and after some time he could not help telling me about how he admired Chiao Kuei, about how faithfully Chiao was serving the co-op. But he still could not see eye to eye with Chiao about that chestnut!

"The animal is old and terribly thin. You can't make it young again," he said.

6

That night after Chiao Kuei had made up a bed for me, he went out to care for his chestnut. I started reading and had finished half the book, but he was still not back. I put on my coat and walked out to find him. From the threshing field came the sound of cutting straw. There, in the moonlight, were Chiao Kuei and a girl pressing the blade of the straw-cutter. The girl would be Kuei Jung. As they did not need a third person, I went back to the house to sleep.

I woke about midnight. The light was still on. Chiao Kuei was reading so intently that he did not notice that I had wakened. He had shaded the lamp to prevent the light from bothering me.

"It's late. You should sleep now," I reminded him.

Only then did he close his book and smile apologetically to me. He went out to feed the animal again, and I picked up the book to see what he was reading so intently. It was a veterinarian's manual.

Several times during the night Chiao Kuei got up to give the horse more fodder. Then, before daybreak when I opened my eyes, he was gone, having neatly made his bed. When I stepped out of the house, the cattle pen was spick and span. Neither Chiao nor the chestnut was to be seen.

Noontime, after I had lunched at the co-op chairman's home, I returned to Chiao Kuei's to pick up something I had left there. On the way I met Chiao giving the chestnut a good wash and currying it with a big comb. Perspiring all over, he said to me, "Comrade Liang, I've found out the cause of its trouble!"

I had never seen him so happy in the days I had known him. I went up to hear what he was going to tell me.

"Last night I read that book on treating animal diseases. It says that an animal grows thin not merely because it is poorly fed, but often because it is infested with lice. Today I took a close look. It's full of lice. They've sucked its blood and eaten off its hair. No wonder it's thin! I'm delousing it, feeding it well and giving it good care. You'll see it fat in no time!"

Meanwhile Fu-shun and the team leader, Li Yung, came over gaily with the brown mule behind them. As soon as it saw Chiao Kuei, it raised its head and brayed. It got free of the rein in Fu-shun's hand, ran towards Chiao Kuei and licked his hand. When Fu-shun came over to catch it, it ran away. Fu-shun gave chase. It ran faster. Fu-shun stopped. It also stopped, raised its head and brayed as if in challenge. Fu-shun got angry and began to whip it right and left.

"Stop!" shouted Chiao Kuei. "Whipping won't help. Let me handle it." And he called the mule by the name he had given it, "Golden Chrysanthemum, come for your fodder!"

The mule docilely answered the call and came over. Chiao Kuei handed over the rein to Fu-shun, who led it away without saying a word.

Li Yung, watching the scene, said, "Chiao Kuei, this animal has a good feeling towards you. I think you should have it."

Chiao Kuei shook his head.

Li Yung turned solemn. "A fine fellow you are, Chiao Kuei," he said. "You complained to the co-op chairman against me about a small matter. For that I was criticized. But I don't mind. I'll correct my mistake once I know what it is. From now on I'll give full support to the way you do things. Beginning tomorrow we shall deliver the manure, first to the foot of Peach Bloom Hill. As usual, we shall arrange for one cart and one animal to be driven by one man, seven carts a day, each cart carrying seven piles of manure. What about your cart and animal?"

"What do *you* say?" Chiao asked in return.

Li Yung looked at the lean chestnut and laughed. "Well, you've given your word. You want to do as much as the others. If we don't allow you to do so, you may think we look down on you, and you may again make a report that we are dampening your enthusiasm."

Chiao Kuei put his hand on the back of the chestnut, which lowered its head and switched its tail. "I'll do as required," he said firmly.

The team leader paled slightly. "Be careful," he warned. "Don't work the animal to death. You'll disgrace yourself that way."

Chiao Kuei said nothing but, biting his lips while taking up the water bucket, led the chestnut away.

The day before I left the village, the transport team leader reported to the co-op chairman on his work. Hsiao Yung-shun asked him who among his team members had done the best. Li Yung had to say, with some embarrassment, that it was Chiao Kuei.

Hsiao and I were amazed. We decided to go to the field the next morning to see how Chiao worked.

It was an enchanting spring morning on the farm. Wild geese flew in formation amidst white clouds in a sky of blue. Peach and pear blossoms brightened the river bank beneath swaying willows, a light breeze scattering the pink and white petals on to the blue stream, which carried them away. The fields were green, either with turf dotted with small wild flowers, or with wheat sprouts, all nodding with dew and seeming to smile.

Suddenly we heard the trotting of a horse behind and, turning to look, saw a cart coming from the direction of the village. Rubber-tyred and polished so it shone, it was fully loaded with black manure. In the shafts was a lean and ugly chestnut horse, and beside the left shaft a man pulling on a rope tied to the cart.

"Oh, so this is how he does it!" I could not help crying out.

Hsiao Yung-shun ran up to him. "Chiao Kuei," he exclaimed, "you can't work like that. I know how you feel, but I can't let you strain yourself!"

Chiao stopped, raised his flushed face and said slowly, "Co-op chairman, I'm not doing this because I'm bull-headed, but in order to complete the job of delivering the manure so that spring sowing can be done in time. Also to make the chestnut strong again. I am in good health. Please don't worry about me."

In the end the two of us helped him by pushing the cart from behind till we reached the field.

At noon that day I left the "East Is Red" Co-op.

Six months passed. Now I was sitting at the window of the stable inn waiting for Chiao Kuei. Staring at the yellow chrysanthemums growing there I wondered if Chiao Kuei's chestnut was still alive.

It was noon but Chiao Kuei was not back yet, so I decided to go to the market and look for him. As I set out I met Chiao and Fu-shun.

Chiao Kuei was leading a sleek chestnut out of the crowd. My heart chilled. The lean chestnut must have died. Otherwise why should he have bought this one? I went up to him and asked, "How much did you pay for the horse?"

"This? Why, 30 yuan," said Chiao smiling and admiring the fine-looking animal.

"Thirty yuan?" I smiled back, incredulous. "Maybe enough for shoeing it!"

"That's right. Only 30 yuan," Fu-shun put in. When you were here last spring, didn't you see me insisting on selling this chestnut? It has been fed by our expert Chiao to become what it is now!"

I could not believe my eyes and ears as I could find no trace of the old chestnut. I walked round it twice to take a close look. Its mane was dark red, eyes dark and shining, a red tassel at its forelock, long tail behind a round rump, legs like pillars, hoofs like plates. This was the horse that would sell for only 30 yuan and was destined for the slaughter house. Quite a different animal now!

I got on Chiao Kuei's cart. Fu-shun rode with us, leaving his own cart to follow behind. With much feeling he said to me, "Comrade Liang, Chiao Kuei has done everything to bring new life to this animal. It has taken me six months to see I was wrong. . . ."

At this he drew my attention to Chiao Kuei's white towel with the words "model co-op member" embroidered on it.

"Splendid! Chiao Kuei's achievements have been recognized!" And I clapped my hands.

Fu-shun continued, "His experience has been reported in the newspapers, and he's been to Shunyi County to popularize his method. His labour has enabled our co-op alone to save the purchase of more than 40 animals, which means a lot of money. He is now the leader of our transport team."

"What about that man Li?" I asked.

"You mean Li Yung?" Fu-shun said with contempt. "He practically ruined our team. His waste of fodder alone made one shudder. He was sent to other work some time ago."

Laughing, Fu-shun said again, "By the way, Comrade Liang, I've happy news for you. Chiao Kuei and Kuei Jung were married three days ago. There's still time for you to pay them a wedding call."

Peking, January 31, 1957

Shepherd's Apprentice

IMMEDIATELY upon his arrival at the agricultural co-operative, Hsia Ching-miao asked the co-op chairman to let him serve as apprentice under Tu Chun-feng.

Ching-miao had never met Tu, but had heard a lot about him from his father. Tu was the co-op's old shepherd, he was told, and much respected throughout the village. Younger people never called him by any other name than "Uncle Tu." Fifty-seven years old, the man had not passed a day away from his flock in the past half century. Toil and suffering marked the greater part of his life, but it had tempered him so that he turned out to be a man of marked ability in his work. The villagers said he had a treasure box for a brain. Everybody knew that any sheep, no matter how scrawny, grew fat after a month under his care. And, as for animal diseases, Uncle Tu's cures were well known, for his long experience enabled him to diagnose even unusual animal troubles after a little observation. Among his admirers was the surgeon of the county veterinary station, who often travelled 40 *li* to call on him for help.

The shepherd's story, as told by Ching-miao's father, had left a deep impression on the boy, and aroused in him a respect for the man and a love for his work. So when the question of going to the countryside for farming practice came up and he decided to go, he thought of Uncle Tu and hoped to become his apprentice.

To his great joy, the co-op chairman granted his request at once and immediately sent the bookkeeper to inform Uncle Tu of Ching-miao's arrival.

He took his bedding roll and satchel happily and followed the chairman out of the co-op office. This was the first day of his new life — the termination of his student days, and the beginning of his life as a shepherd. He determined to work hard and learn all he could of this old peasant's valuable experience, to digest and develop it. He would note down for publication what was in the master's treasure box. Ching-miao already saw in his mind's eye the carcasses of mutton and bales of wool produced for the state through his own labour as a specialist in animal husbandry. This was what he would like to be all his life. . . .

With these thoughts he imagined that everything, even the trees and the hills, was smiling at him. Even the crunch of the pebbles underfoot sounded like the staccato of music to his ears.

He turned to the co-op chairman and found the latter looking at him intently.

Ching-miao was no stranger to the chairman either, for he and Ching-miao's father had borne arms together in the early revolutionary war days. The coming of the son of an old comrade to work in his co-op delighted him, and at the same time gave him a feeling of heavy responsibility.

"Ching-miao," he began in all earnestness, "you mustn't forget what your father has told you. Things aren't as simple as young people may imagine. A school graduate like you has to be tried and tempered in order to become a real peasant, especially a new peasant with socialist consciousness. . . ."

"Co-op chairman," Ching-miao interposed, "you needn't worry about me on that score. I won't flinch before any difficulty. I'll never bring disgrace to my father, or to my school."

The co-op chairman nodded approval and smiled. "Uncle Tu has quite a temper sometimes," he went on. "You may find him fiery in the beginning, but once you get to understand him well enough you'll respect him from the bottom of your heart. You'll have to be modest, hard working and obedient, though. He hates to see a frivolous person."

Ching-miao nodded understandingly.

They walked through a grove of date trees and came to a compound. Entering the barred gate they saw a large ground. Along the wall on the north side was a row of sheep folds with openings facing the sun, and to the west lay a cottage with a low thatched roof. The window was partially open, and thin smoke coiled into the space outside. They heard some people talking in the room.

"Well, don't look so peevish, Uncle Tu. This time you'll have a commissioner's son as apprentice. A high school graduate, too!"

"Stop your nonsense, will you? This is no joke. I simply won't have it!"

By now Ching-miao and the co-op chairman were close enough to the window for the latter to shout through it. "Uncle Tu," he called, "Ching-miao is here!"

There was no answer, and they went in.

It was a big room. Against the wall on the south side was a *kang* heated by a stove of the same height at one end. A hurricane lantern, a whip and a canteen hung on the wall. A man of around thirty leaned on the bed, while on the outer edge sat one who looked to be in his fifties. The older man seemed short of stature, due perhaps to his slightly hunched back. Set in his long, narrow face was a pair of small, shining eyes. His jacket was of home-spun, blue in colour, the wide overlap of which had brass buttons in buttonholes on the left side. At his waist was a black girdle, and the soles of his cloth shoes were closely hobnailed. The costume looked strange to Ching-miao, but he found it attractive, for it made the man look hale and hearty. The man received them with knit eye-brows, not even bothering to look up but puffing continually at his pipe in displeasure. This was the old shepherd, obviously. Ching-miao extended his hand to him, asking if he was not indeed "Uncle Tu."

It was the co-op chairman who answered. "Right, this is Uncle Tu. And this is Hsia Ching-miao. You two will work together from now on."

Uncle Tu took the pipe from between his teeth, but there was no change in his expression. He responded to Ching-miao's extended hand with only a quick glance at it and said, "Just sit down." Turning to the co-op chairman, he went on, "Look, our sheep don't need two men to handle them. It would be better to assign the student to some other team!"

The co-op chairman was surprised and asked, "Weren't you yourself asking for more help, since the job is too much for one man? Why the sudden change of mind?"

"Uncle Tu," Ching-miao joined in, stepping closer to him, "I've come here to be your apprentice, to learn from you. I won't do anything else, but stay right here with you."

"Eh," sighed Uncle Tu, forcing a smile. "A student like you is just not cut out for this kind of job. Day in and day out, rain or shine, you've got to follow the dumb animals over the fields and into the mountain. It's too hard for you. But the co-operative office needs people like you. If you're going to stay, better keep books and things like that. You can do well there, but tending sheep isn't for you."

"I'm sure it isn't easy," agreed Ching-miao, "but hard work's what I want. I'll do whatever you say."

The co-op chairman could see what was troubling Uncle Tu, and he put in a word. "Certainly. I'm sure it's as Ching-miao says. He'll do as you say. Now you'll agree, won't you?"

"Nobody understands this better than I do," Uncle Tu insisted. "I say it just won't do, and that's all there is to it. If I don't state my views plainly now, we'll owe Commissioner Hsia a big apology when things go wrong in the future."

At this moment of the deadlock, a clear voice called outside the window, "Papa, lunch is ready." Following the voice there appeared a girl of about eighteen. Her round face was tanned and rosy, and wreathed in smiles. She was about to say something as she rushed in, but the sight of a stranger stopped her and for a moment she looked puzzled. Then, leaning back against the door, she said in a hushed voice, "It's lunch time, papa."

This gave Uncle Tu an excuse to leave. He rose abruptly, tapped his pipe against the edge of the *kang* and said, "It's no use trying to talk me into it, co-op chairman. Send this student to some other team. Not that I'm unreasonable. It's only for the good of us all." And he stalked out.

2

Hsia Ching-miao was dumbfounded and deeply hurt. He felt like a lively, frolicking lamb that had suddenly knocked its head against a stone wall. The flame of enthusiasm with which he had come was put out by the cold water Uncle Tu poured on it. Disappointed, he sat mute on the edge of the *kang*.

But life is like that. The happiest man has his sad moments. A fortnight ago, Ching-miao had been in no higher spirits than now.

He was in school, and there was a propaganda drive to mobilize the school graduates to work in the countryside. As Ching-miao was a students' association functionary, he had worked with the cadres in the campaign. They had explained to the other students the bright future of China's countryside and the significance of their taking part in rural socialist construction. Ching-miao had himself persuaded several young people to go. Encouraged by the result, he had doubled his propaganda effort.

One day, however, one of the students put a question straight to him: "Ching-miao, you're urging others to go, but how about yourself?"

Ching-miao was unprepared for such a question and could only manage to stammer out, "I . . . I . . . of course . . . but, my father's not at home just now. He's attending a meeting at the provincial capital."

As a matter of fact, Ching-miao liked the countryside. Both his parents were peasants, and he had been born on a farm and had spent his boyhood there. Country life was akin to him, and he had always thought of going back to the countryside as an agronomist — *after* graduating from high school and then college, where he would study agriculture. But to go *now* and give up his plan for a college education, to work as an ordinary peasant, well, he was really not prepared for that.

From that day on his troubled feelings had got him down, and no one ever saw him do any propaganda work again.

Presently Ching-miao's father returned and phoned to let the boy know he was back. Ching-miao hurried home.

No sooner had he entered the room than his father asked, "Have you thought yet about going to the countryside, son, now that there's this drive going on in your school?"

"No, I haven't."

"Why not?"

The dialogue ended there, and the father did not press further, but talked about other things.

However, he came back to the subject later on, asking, "Ching-miao, have you forgotten about Mama Liu?"

"No, father, how could I forget her?" Ching-miao replied, wondering why his father raised this question, as if he could ever forget Mama Liu. He felt he was grossly misunderstood.

Ching-miao owed his very life to Mama Liu. When he was only two months old, his mother had to carry him when she followed the main force of the Eighth Route Army to another place. That was during the hardest year of fighting against Japanese aggression in northern Hopei Province. It was pitch dark at night, and the troops were on a forced march. The enemy was pursuing them; there were fires all around and shooting behind. With the baby in her arms, Ching-miao's mother could not keep up. Still she refused other comrades' offers of help, for it would add to their burden. What was she to do with her baby? Just then a native woman who acted as guide for the troops came over to her, took the baby from her arms and said, "Comrade, we're near my home village. Let me take the baby. I'll bring it up even if you never pass this way again. I'll never abandon it no matter what difficulties there may be."

From that time on Ching-miao was cared for by this kind woman, Mama Liu, in her two-room thatched house at the river bank. She worked hard to clothe the baby, often spinning and weaving far into the night after a long day of other work. For feeding, she asked nursing mothers to spare some milk and, in rain or wind, would nestle the baby in her arms and go out to collect it.

Misfortune befell the village in 1948 when the Kuomintang reactionary troops invaded it in their offensive against the liberated areas. Ching-miao's father was the secretary of the county committee of the Communist Party, and the local reactionaries knew about it. They plotted to get hold of the child so as to win an award from their superiors. The village was surrounded in the search for the boy, whom Mama Liu had hidden in a cellar. The enemy seized her and demanded that she hand over the child, lashing her with a wet whip; but she said nothing. They tempted her with a basketful of silver dollars, but she ignored it. Finally the beasts set fire to her house and threw her into the flames. As the fire enveloped her, she was still calling Ching-miao's name.

The incident was indelible in Ching-miao's mind; it seared into his heart. He could not remember his father mentioning it except at a time of crisis, and that had been only once since they'd come into the city after the liberation. He was in primary school then and had fallen in with bad companions so that he lost interest in school. At that time his father said to him, "How is it that you're behaving so badly! Don't you ever think of your responsibility to Mama Liu, who died for you?" Ching-miao had cried then, and the next morning he took his satchel and went off to school. That year he became first in his class and a member of the Youth League. Now that his father had mentioned Mama Liu again, he realized what he ought to do. His heart beat fast.

Then his father said sternly, "You want to go to college. That's not a bad thing. However, since you plan to study agriculture, you ought to do some farming before you can become an agronomist. You shouldn't look down on being a peasant. It was a peasant who saved you with her life. Now that the building up of the countryside needs you, why should you hold back?"

Ching-miao didn't cry this time, but spent a sleepless night and went to school in the morning to sign up to go to the countryside.

Now he was finding himself unwanted here. Why was there such a difference between the attitude of his father, the teachers and the Youth League, and the attitude of Uncle Tu? One side called on the students to become the first generation of educated peasants, and told them that they were much needed in the countryside. The other gave him such a cold shoulder.

3

It was a hot, muggy summer afternoon. Not a leaf of the mulberry tree outside the window was stirring. The cicadas chirped continually, setting Ching-miao all the more on edge.

He was left alone in the room, which only aggravated his vexation. He was looking at the floor, lost in thought, when suddenly he was aware of the aroma of hot food. He looked up and saw a girl standing right in front of him.

She had an enamel food container in her hand, and was looking at him with eyes that sparkled with warmth. She put the food on the *kang* and said, "Come and eat now."

It occurred to Ching-miao that this was the girl who had called Uncle Tu home for lunch, and he quickly got to his feet.

"I'm not hungry," he said. "Besides, the co-op chairman said I'm to have my meals with the book-keepers."

"Why with them?" she queried, pouting. "Hurry and eat this. And take off your jacket. You're running with sweat!"

Ching-miao felt his jacket. It was sopping wet. He smiled awkwardly and took it off.

"We heard you were coming a few days ago," the girl went on, "and we're delighted. We'll be in the same Youth League branch here and you'll feel at home. Let me know if you need anything. My name's Tu Chuan. Uncle Tu is my father. I'm responsible for the Youth League in our co-operative, and the co-op chairman has just given me your letter of introduction from the League organization. We'll be in the same group. And I might as well tell you now that I haven't much of a school education and am looking forward to your helping me."

The friendliness of the girl moved and encouraged Ching-miao, and he perked up again. He felt hungry, too, and heartily enjoyed the meal of millet with beans and a dish of fresh vegetable.

Tu Chuan, who sat facing him while he ate, said, "For the time being I'll bring your meals here for you, but later my parents can arrange for you to eat at our house. There are just the three of us in the family."

The thought of this arrangement so jolted the boy that a mouthful of millet stuck in his throat and he had to force it down. He screwed up his face and said, "But your father won't even have me as his apprentice. How can I come to your house and eat at the same table with him. What if he kicks me out the first day!"

Tu Chuan was amused. "See what a terror you take him to be!" she said. "Why don't you go around a bit and find out whether my father has ever kicked anybody out of the house? Never mind his harsh talk. That's just one of his ways, and you'll have to go deeper than that to know what he really thinks. He's likely watching for your reactions too, seeing if you have the qualities the work takes."

At that Ching-miao put down his chopsticks and jumped to his feet, exclaiming, "Is that so? Why didn't you tell me sooner? I was really worried!"

Tu Chuan became serious. "Finish your meal. We'll go to the League branch meeting. The Party secretary and the co-op chairman will both be there and we'll tell you all about the co-op. You can say whatever you want too — make your requests, tell us your ideas — and we'll see what we can do."

After Ching-miao finished eating, Tu Chuan collected the container and chopsticks and they left for the meeting.

Outside the yard and having crossed the sweet potato field, they were about to turn into the village when they saw Uncle Tu grazing his flock on the far river bank. He also saw them but turned his head, flourished his whip and drove the sheep into the aspen grove where he vanished from sight.

4

As Uncle Tu drove the flock through the woods he felt strangely uncomfortable. The tree tops were bathed in the slanting rays of the afternoon sun and the dense aspen leaves, reflecting the sunlight, shone as if they had been silvered. And when a sudden breeze blew through them they danced as though joyfully, while under the trees the fat sheep grazed eagerly on the patches of lush grass.

Uncle Tu was convinced that to have more sheep of better strains required people who knew how to breed and care for the animals. Also that sheep raising was a side-occupation adding considerably to the collective's income. Actually, the brigade's flock was growing steadily, but there had not been any new people for this work. He had thought for a long time about teaching a few new, good hands to prepare for larger flocks in the future, and he considered this training as a contribution he could make to the co-operative.

In fact, in the co-op's second year he had accepted as apprentice a youngster named Tu Teh-sheng, one of his grand-nephews.

Tu Teh-sheng had gone to live with an aunt in the city to study in a primary school there. Failing in the middle school entrance examination after sixth grade, he came back to the village and idled away his time at home. The village and Youth League branch cadres persuaded him to work in the co-op. He was offered an apprenticeship under his grand-uncle, which he accepted with great reluctance. Uncle Tu, however, was pleased, and their kinship increased his enthusiasm. He was eager to teach the boy everything he knew, to see him become a good sheep man in the shortest time possible.

But Teh-sheng looked down on sheep herding and took the job only as something to tide him over until a better opportunity turned up. His thoughts were always miles away from the sheep, to say nothing of doing what was expected of him. He would not even bother to take a whip with him out herding, though he never failed to take along a thermos and some cakes. He would play a mouth-organ along the way till he stumbled over a sheep, and was forever complaining about aches and pains. This was all very annoying to Uncle Tu. Besides, when it was time for the sheep to rest, Teh-sheng would spread a blanket on the ground, lie down and go to sleep after a hearty snack, leaving the flock unattended. Back home in the evening, he would read novels far into the night and never get up in the morning without people pounding on his door to wake him. Even then he would appear still half asleep and grumbling. Behind Uncle Tu's back he called the old sheep man "pig-headed," "backward," "stick-in-the-mud," "selfish," etc., and Uncle Tu had exercised great restraint with this "apprentice" of his, till finally his patience was exhausted.

One day, as a last straw, Teh-sheng played a prank on Uncle Tu. They were out with the flock when the boy, tired of his mouth-organ playing, pulled Uncle Tu to the side of a buckwheat field and, mimicking a high-brow city accent, said, "Grand-uncle, may I ask what that is over there with a red stem, green leaves and white flowers?" The jest was more than Uncle Tu could take — to think of the boy with his short experience of city life becoming so highfalutin as to pretend he no longer recognized buckwheat. The old man threw the youngster to the ground and began raining blows on him with his whip and shouting with each stroke, "This is what it is! This is what it is!"

The boy became alarmed and cried desperately, "Grand-uncle, are you going to beat me to death in this buckwheat field!"

Uncle Tu couldn't help laughing when he saw the boy drop his pretence so quickly. "See what a hypocrite you are!" he reproved. "It takes only a good hiding to make you remember what buckwheat is!"

The incident gave Teh-sheng the excuse he needed to quit the work, and nobody could persuade him to stay on. He was determined to go back to the city and find work there.

As for Uncle Tu, he realized he was wrong to give way to his irritation and strike the boy, and he voluntarily criticized himself at the co-op members' general meeting.

And that was how he and his first apprentice had parted.

The incident had distressed Uncle Tu for a long time. He drew a conclusion from it. Whenever the question of taking another apprentice came up, he would sigh and say, "Young people nowadays are different from what they were in our time. They have no idea what hunger and cold are. They don't know the taste of hardship. Really, how can they learn anything? I won't go looking for trouble any more."

In the following couple of years, however, people were sent by both the prefecture and the county to help him sum up his experience, which they had put into print. As Uncle Tu could not read, he had it read to him, but oddly enough, his summary sounded confusing even to himself. From this he drew another conclusion: The best way to pass his experience on to others was through personal contact on the job, and that would be for him to take another apprentice.

But the two conclusions contradicted each other, a situation that had tortured him right up until the time Hsia Ching-miao came onto the scene.

Towards noon on the day of Ching-miao's arrival, Uncle Tu was rounding up the sheep under the shade of a grove of trees at the river bank for a rest when he saw the bookkeeper approaching. As soon as Tu was within hearing distance, he began in a loud voice, "Uncle Tu, hurry back to the sheep-fold compound. The co-op chairman's got a fine apprentice for you. He's the son of the commissioner and a high school graduate. You're sure to be pleased with your apprentice this time. Go now. I'll look after the flock for you."

Uncle Tu had heard from his daughter about the young man's coming and he had immediately clapped his hand on his knee and said approvingly, "Everything is different in our new society, and Communists are selfless. In the old days, a ranking official's kin had easy access to a comfortable post and a commissioner's son would have half of his father's status. Who would ever have dreamt of his becoming a peasant!" But now when he heard that this young man was going to be his apprentice, a feeling of vague misgiving came to the fore. He thought of his experience with Tu Teh-sheng. Wasn't this boy likely to be even worse than his predecessor? Teh-sheng had been only two years in the city, while this new one had grown up there. Also, Teh-sheng had only a primary school education while this one was a high school graduate. And besides, Teh-sheng was a relative of his, while this one was not, to say nothing of the new boy's being the son of a high functionary. Certainly the young fellow would not be happy herding sheep! How could he teach a young man who would likely not co-operate with him and carry out his orders? Besides, he had never been one to coddle or fawn on anybody, so in dealing with such a person he would have to weigh every word carefully or there would be nothing but trouble.

And this was why the old sheep man reacted as he did when Ching-miao was introduced to him.

The co-op chairman had followed him to his house and told him what the commissioner had said when he entrusted his son to the co-operative. Uncle Tu had replied that the commissioner was a good functionary, and that as a matter of fact he had voted for him at the last election of deputies to the People's Congress. But this was another thing. Young people today were just too delicate. He reminded the co-op chairman of the situation with Teh-sheng and said he wouldn't do it again even if he was called a pig-headed old man.

"But the young people have made headway in these two years," the co-op chairman had said. "And an old calendar won't give you new dates. What makes you so sure that Ching-miao is no good?"

"I don't have any evidence, but. . . ."

"So give him a break then. If he really can't do the job, we'll discuss the question again. How about that?"

Uncle Tu had agreed, but his mind was still not at ease.

5

After his talk with the co-op chairman, Uncle Tu went back to his sheep and spent the whole afternoon in the aspen grove. Not until sunset did he slowly drive his flock home.

On reaching the compound, he was going to open the gate of the sheep-fold as usual to let the sheep in when he found it already wide open, so that the animals went in without trouble. Then suddenly there appeared a tall, slim young fellow in a white shirt. He was carrying two basketfuls of sheep manure suspended from a shoulder pole, which made him lurch along. Though the lad's back was bent, his neck protruded and his mouth was open as he gasped for breath, Uncle Tu recognized him as Hsia Ching-miao. He was impressed by the sight, and by the way Ching-miao gripped the pole as if afraid it might get away from him.

"So you're back, Uncle Tu," Ching-miao called out between gasps.

"Um," Uncle Tu nodded, keeping his long face as he went on herding the sheep into the fold.

Ching-miao had cleaned the fold. Not only had the manure been removed, but a layer of loose, new earth had been laid in its place. Even the sheep seemed to notice something different. Uncle Tu had been in the habit of clearing out the manure after the flock was in the fold, and he could only do it by herding the sheep to one side, cleaning the other, and then herding them back again while he finished the job. The operation took so long that he was never on time for supper, and his daughter had to call him several times.

The clean sheep-fold pleased the old man. Closing the gate in the fence after him, he walked behind Ching-miao, who was carrying out the last load of manure. But when Ching-miao got to a pile of night-soil, he dumped the manure there, a mistake that excited Uncle Tu to exclaim "Ai-ya-ya!" "Why did you dump the sheep manure on the night-soil pile?" he demanded. "They have different uses and can't be mixed. Can't you see the sheep dung pile on the west side?"

No sooner had the old man said this than it occurred to him that his manner was too harsh. Yet mollification was quite beyond him. Fearing that this young son of a functionary might make a scene, he hurried away immediately.

Ching-miao's cheeks were burning with the sting of the reproach. Fortunately, there had been the League branch meeting, which had helped him to understand matters that had disturbed him before. Now, instead of just feeling offended, he searched within himself for the cause of the blunder.

He recalled how Tu Chuan, friendly as she was, had criticized him in that very first meeting. "Why should you make the one-sided demand on others to treat you warmly?" she asked. "Why not look within yourself and see how you should behave? Are you not still burdened with the thinking that you're an educated young man, and that you're a cut above us in status too? If you don't change your attitude, how can you expect people to accept you?"

Ching-miao had at first found Tu Chuan's words hard to take, but on second thoughts he began to feel thankful for them. Especially when she had asked him right out,

"Did you come because you wanted to, because you felt you ought to, or was it because you felt you had to, since the Party had issued the call and your father had urged you?" That was really the question, now that he was made to think of it.

At the meeting, Tu Chuan had talked also about her father, and admitted her mistake of neglecting to talk to him beforehand so that he might have received Ching-miao better. She then suggested ways of improving the situation. After the meeting she had gone with Ching-miao to the sheep-fold and explained to him how her father did the work there.

Ching-miao's enthusiasm had mounted, and he only wished he could get everything done at once. Thinking back, he realized that had he been more careful and asked Tu Chuan where to dump the sheep manure, the mistake would not have happened. He regretted his own negligence and rashness, realizing these to be inimical to his learning from Uncle Tu. Then he hurried to remove all the misplaced manure and dump it where it belonged.

The crescent of a new moon hung over the mulberry in the yard, and it seemed especially quiet. Uncle Tu stepped quietly in, his pipe in his hand. He made his way to the fence where he picked up the shovel, baskets and shoulder pole, then started towards the night-soil compost, thinking to remove the sheep manure. But the first few shovelfuls yielded none, and he looked closer. There really wasn't any left! He went to the manure pit. There was more sheep manure there than the day before, but the top was as flat as ever, with a layer of loose, new earth over it. It was just as though he had done it himself. He stood there for a moment, thinking. Then he went back to the fence and replaced the tools. Drawing at his pipe, he looked at the sheep. They were sleeping peacefully.

The cool night breeze carried to him the pleasant scent of the new hay. The moon had climbed high into the sky, and he finally decided it was bed-time.

As he pulled open the door to his room, he noticed a lighted insecticide rope hanging from the ceiling. In summer, he usually lit one each evening against mosquitoes, but tonight, in all the confusion, he had clean forgotten about it. When he struck a match and lit the lamp, he saw Ching-miao already asleep there while his own bedding had been arranged. On the farther end of the *kang* was a teapot with a cloth around it to keep it warm. Though not particularly thirsty, Uncle Tu drank two bowls of the warm brew one after the other, in appreciation of the kindness. Light perspiration appeared on his forehead, and he felt very happy.

Ching-miao had kicked off his coverlet, exposing his bare body curled up in slumber. Uncle Tu climbed onto the *kang* and gently pulled the cover over the boy as he said to himself, "Let's see how you'll make out in the hills tomorrow."

6

Uncle Tu woke up at the break of dawn. Rising before the sun was his lifetime habit, and he invariably woke up punctually, no matter how late he had gone to bed. Now he would awaken Ching-miao. "Let's get up," he called. "We'll go to the hills today." But there was nobody in the boy's bedding, which had all been folded up.

The previous day's hard work had exhausted Ching-miao so that by night he had fallen asleep almost as soon as his head hit the pillow. But, thinking of the work to be done the next day, he had awakened when it was still pitch dark and, careful not to disturb Uncle Tu, had gotten up quietly, tidied up his bedding and stolen out of the room with his clothes under his arm, to get dressed in the yard. Then he took the big broom and swept the whole yard clean, after which he drew and carried water from the well to sprinkle the ground and fill the big water trough at the sheep-fold fence. He was about to open the fence gate and let the sheep out to drink when he stopped short. For it occurred to him that though mules and horses were watered in the morning, he did not know if sheep were. He decided to ask Uncle Tu first, not to be careless again.

He leaned against the fence looking at the animals which were awake even earlier than he. As darkness gradually gave way to the morning glow and the roof of the shed turned rosy in the first rays of the sun, the sheep jerked to their feet one after another, stretched their necks towards Ching-miao and baaed, as if in welcome. Ching-miao stroked and caressed them gladly as he would be close to the sheep from that day on. He would take them to the greenest pastures every day and drive them home each night with their bellies full. In spring he would be busy with the lambing, in summer with the shearing of bale after bale of wool. Autumn would be the time to ship the fattened-up sheep to the city. . . . This would be his contribution to the state, the joy of his youth.

"You got up early!" It was Uncle Tu.

"Not too early. I'm just up."

Uncle Tu, seeing that the entire place had been cleaned up, nodded. "Go and wash up for breakfast now. We'll go to the hills today," he said.

After breakfast, Uncle Tu took from the wall a leather whip with a long handle and handed it to Ching-miao, saying, "Take this with you."

The simple act made Ching-miao feel like a recruit being given his gun. His heart beat faster.

The trail they came out onto looked like a long cord with one end in the clouds and the other lying at the foot of the mountain. Along the upper part of the trail were precipices shading the sky. Mammoth rocks in grotesque shapes protruded and looked suspended in the air, as if they might come crashing down at any moment. Ravines flanking the trail below appeared bottomless, dark and frightening. Ching-miao proceeded cautiously.

Presently he felt his legs weaken and begin to shake. He furtively rubbed one calf and cursed it. "Useless! I'm not frightened. Why should you be shaking so?" he addressed his leg. He saw Uncle Tu striding along from one rock to the next, as nimble as the sheep and steadier than he would be on a paved road. He saw to the west a better foot path uphill and figured that Uncle Tu had purposely taken the more difficult one to try him.

By the time they reached the other side of the mountain Ching-miao's clothes were limp with perspiration.

Near noon, they came to a big patch of flat land where they rounded up the sheep in a shaded spot to rest them. Then Ching-miao followed Uncle Tu into the shade of a big tree where they too rested and had their lunch.

After eating, Uncle Tu lit his pipe and began smoking, when he spotted black clouds gathering in the northeastern sky. He sprang to his feet and cried, "Hurry! A storm's coming!"

Ching-miao jumped up, grasped his long-handled whip and asked, "What was that, Uncle Tu?"

"Look, there's going to be a storm!"

The sun was still strong overhead, how could there be a storm? Ching-miao thought. But a violent wind soon howled through the valley, carrying the dark clouds, now growing rapidly, towards them.

"What shall we do? Are sheep afraid of the rain?" Ching-miao asked agitatedly.

"After the sheep have had warm grass and warm water, it's dangerous to expose them to rain. They'll get sick, or lose a lot of weight. Let's hurry and get them into the nearest cave over there."

They picked up the few things on the ground and made for the cave, driving the flock ahead of them. Ching-miao was so anxious that he paid no attention to a pebble in his shoe, nor to the thorns that tore at his trousers and drew blood from his legs. He forgot everything except the urgency of getting the sheep into the cave. If only he had a bag big enough to put the whole flock into and carry them to safety!

They hadn't driven the flock far before the gale was upon them and big raindrops pelted down. Nothing could be seen in the distance but a white haze, and the ominous sound of the approaching downpour grew louder. Ching-miao cried excitedly to Uncle Tu, "What shall we do with the sheep in the storm?"

But Uncle Tu remained calm. "There's a small cave over there," he said, pointing with his whip. "We'll take shelter in it."

The cave was under overhanging rocks and was a little more than the height of a man at the entrance, but lower and narrower further in. They packed as many of the sheep in as they could, but still a few remained exposed outside.

"I'll stay outside to keep these sheep from straying," Uncle Tu said. "You get in. Hurry!"

"A young fellow can stand a soaking better than an older one," Ching-miao responded. "Better go in yourself." And he helped Uncle Tu get a foothold inside the cave.

The downpour came, with stones carried by its force down the slopes, and bushes flattened under its lashing. The small cave which had promised shelter was no longer safe, as the wind changed direction and not only the sheep near the entrance were soaked, but the whole place would soon be flooded. Only then did Ching-miao think of the waterproof sheeting he had with him. He unfolded it and tried to cover the backs of the sheep with it, but the wind blew it off. He jumped onto a rock and held the cloth up by the two top corners so that it covered the opening of the cave and screened off the raindrops, though he got wet through.

Uncle Tu was impressed with the youngster's forgetting himself in order to protect the flock, and thought that now at last he had found someone whose devotion and sense of duty in caring for the sheep matched his. This was a new thing in his long life as a shepherd.

So he got onto the rock to take turns holding up the waterproof cloth. The two carried on the fight against the storm till the sky cleared.

7

By evening it was clear enough for the moon to show on the horizon. The air was pure and refreshing.

Uncle Tu stepped out of the co-op chairman's house and headed for the sheep-fold compound. It was very still there. A light flickered in his room, casting the profile of a sturdy young man at the window. What a welcome change this was from the gloomy solitude that had prevailed at the fold. Now, this was broken. The compound sprang to life, as warm as his own house.

In the hours Uncle Tu had worked with this city boy, he had been giving him what amounted to an entrance examination — an unwritten test. The boy had passed the test, and Uncle Tu was very happy that he had now a real apprentice.

The old sheep man walked up to the door and pulled it open. There was Ching-miao, sitting in the lamplight with a basin of water, clipping at the blisters on his feet with a pair of scissors. He was so absorbed in his task that he failed to notice Uncle Tu there until the old sheep man stalked heavily across the room.

Ching-miao, embarrassed, hurried to hide his feet. But Uncle Tu had already seen the blisters, the beads of

Illustration by Tung Chen-sheng

Sending In Vegetable Seed

IN the last few days, Meng Chao-hsien had become restless waiting for a letter. She had even lost her appetite.

A girl of nineteen, tall and slender with oval face, clear eyes and fine arched eyebrows, she was leader of the vegetable growing group. Her long plaits tied with bright red wool seemed to add to her liveliness as she dashed into the courtyard, face red, forehead and nose beaded with perspiration, to ask, "Any letters for me today, mum?"

Before her mother could answer, the women who were visiting the Mengs smiled. Chao-hsien laughed happily and seized her mother's arm. "Give it to me, mum, quick," she urged. "I'm sure there's a letter."

The mother gave Chao-hsien a reproachful look. "They're laughing because you're such a flighty girl — always rushing about. Letter? Who should be writing you a letter?"

Chao-hsien frowned, then in a moment asked, "Has the postman been here? He stops in for a drink of water every time he passes our village. Have you seen him today?"

40

"No, I haven't seen him today, Chao-hsien. Don't. . . ." But the girl had flitted out again.

Mrs Fang looked at the disappearing figure of Chao-hsien and smiled. "I never knew your daughter had a boy friend," she said. "But ever since she came back from buying vegetable seed at the fair, I've noticed she's been restless, always looking for a letter."

"Chao-hsien is a smart girl," put in Mrs Li. "You don't have to worry; she's sure to find you a good son-in-law."

Mrs Meng listened calmly to her neighbours' comments. It was only natural for a mother to think about her daughter's marriage. She hadn't worried, because she knew the girl was sensible. Still, in the last few days, she had to admit, her daughter was really acting abnormally. Mrs Meng felt rather upset, a little put out even, with the young man. Why didn't he write? Why should he make her daughter unhappy? Today Chao-hsien seemed unusually anxious. Mrs Meng went to the gate and looked outside. There she was, standing again by the pond where the postman would pass. Her mother sighed.

In the shade of the willow beside the pond, Chao-hsien watched with eager eyes the path which ran westward through the sorghum fields. How she hoped that a green bicycle would appear now, bringing her a pile of letters! But she waited and watched in vain. She counted on her fingers: one day, two days . . . already five days had passed since she had gone to the fair to buy vegetable seed, but again there was no letter. Since every people's commune was expanding its vegetable plots, seed was in great demand. Without seed their plan for a bumper vegetable harvest would be empty talk. Chao-hsien had got a bright idea and had bought a sheet of red paper and borrowed a brush and inkstone from the primary school to write two copies of this "notice":

To all production brigade leaders:

In response to the directive of the Party Central Committee and the State Council, our production brigade wants to expand its autumn vegetable plots. Our problem is — we haven't enough seed. The Commune has provided half of what we need, but that's all we've got, and we haven't been able so far to buy any. Can you help us? If you have any seed to spare, no matter how little, please write to us and we'll go immediately to buy it from you. Thanks in advance!

> Meng Chao-hsien, leader of Meng-chiatan Production Brigade Vegetable Growing Group

She had posted a copy of this notice at each end of the main street of Paochuang Village, then walked home well satisfied. She was sure this would bring her plenty of good seed quicker than if she scoured the countryside on foot or telephoned around inquiring. As soon as she got home she asked her father, who led their brigade, to double their allotment of land for vegetables.

"Aren't you young people wanting to put the cart before the horse?" remarked her father, none too pleased. "How can you plan production like that? You haven't got your seed yet, and you want the land to wait for you. You know it's already sowing time. In seven days it'll be too late. Can you be responsible if that land lies idle?"

"Give me the seven days. If the land's not sown to vegetables, then you can sow your buckwheat." But the girl remained confident.

Now five of the seven days had passed — slowly, yet all too quickly. Chao-hsien was getting worried and was restless. She began to lose her appetite and did not sleep well either. One night she dreamed she was shouldering a sack of seed and woke up laughing. . . .

The production brigade's plan was to provide each member with 500 *jin* of vegetables for the winter and spring, and this was no light task! Chao-hsien felt she must not let the members down; she must carry out the plan. Everything depended on these last two days. Time would not wait. And yet that wretched postman had not come!

It was past noon. The postman would not be coming now. Perhaps someone had already gotten her letters and taken them to the brigade office. So she hurried there, only to find the door locked. She leaned against the window-sill and looked through the screen. There, to her joy, she saw on the desk two letters and four parcels with her name on them. What a windfall! In her excitement, she opened the screen and jumped in through the window instead of fetching the old accountant to open the door. Then, quickly, she took the two letters and four parcels, jumped out, fixed the screen back in place and headed straight for the vegetable plot.

The four parcels were quite a load, but she laughed to herself as she ran. Then she stopped, opened one letter and read it very quickly. It said, "Comrade Meng

43

Chao-hsien: Sorry we haven't much and can only send you one *jin* of vegetable seed. . . . Huatu Production Brigade, Tangwu Commune."

She opened the second letter. It was brief but very moving. It read, "I was keeping this half *jin* of seed for my private plot, but since your production brigade needs it, I'm sending it to you. The collective comes before the individual! Don't worry about my plot. It's only one-fifth of a *mu*, and my neighbours will let me have some seedlings. . . ."

The girl's eyes misted as she pressed the precious parcels to her heart and thought of the comradeliness behind these gifts.

Just then there was a splashing ahead and, from out of a cluster of reeds, a man appeared.

He was carrying a parcel, which he laid on the small stone bridge over the stream. Holding on to a willow branch with one hand, he washed the mud from his feet, after which he casually put on his shoes. Looking up, he saw Chao-hsien and shouted, "Say, comrade, is this Mengchiatan Village?"

The girl always liked to meet people and enjoy a pleasant chat, particularly at this moment when she was so happy. "Yes, it's Mengchiatan all right. Where are you from? Visiting relatives here?"

The young man was tall and slim, with a broad forehead, square jaw and lively, sparkling eyes. "I have no relatives here," he replied. "But I'm looking for somebody. Can you tell me where Comrade Meng Chao-hsien of the vegetable group lives?"

"Looking for me?"

The young man smiled, stepped forward and said warmly, "So you are Comrade Meng. What a coincidence!"

"But . . . who are you?" the girl queried.

"I'm from the Leap Forward Commune of Anchiu County, south of the river," the young man said in a straightforward way. "My name is Wang Yuan-ching. I've brought you some vegetable seed."

Chao-hsien was amazed. Anchiu County was separated from her county of Changlo by the Wenho River. The Leap Forward Commune was more than 30 *li* away. How had the news of Mengchiatan's shortage of vegetable seed travelled so far? And imagine this young commune member coming all this way to deliver it! Too grateful for words, Chao-hsien picked up the young man's package. "This must have caused you a lot of trouble. How can we ever thank you?" she stammered. The package was heavy. "How much did your brigade sow? How is it that you have so much to spare?" she asked, her questions tumbling one onto another.

"The other day I crossed the river into your county to learn how Kaoyai Commune makes chemical fertilizer. I passed by Paochuang Village and saw your notice, and when I went back, I told our brigade leader about it. He immediately asked the storeman to see what seed we had left to send to you. But all our extra vegetable seed had already been shared out to other communes. I knew you must be pretty anxious to get seed, or you wouldn't have put up that notice. So I asked around among our commune members and collected a handful here, another there. In all, I got a little over ten *jin*."

The young man told this as if it were only the natural course of events. But Chao-hsien knew the distance he must have walked, going from house to house to collect this seed, the many requests he must have made, the sweat it must have cost him. This spirit of helping another out of difficulty immediately inspired Chao-hsien's respect for the young man. "You took such pains for us," she said. "You could have written or, at most, mailed the seed to us. But you went to all the trouble of coming yourself."

"I intended to mail the seed to you, but our brigade leader said he had been to your village and knew you didn't have much experience in growing vegetables. So he gave me two days to deliver the seed and explain to you how to sow it."

Chao-hsien clapped her hands together for joy. "You really think of everything!" she exclaimed. "In fact, I was worried. Our vegetable growing group has only just been formed and we've got to learn from scratch. You must be pretty expert in raising vegetables. Come, let's go to the village first. You need a rest!"

The girl's compliment embarrassed the young man. "I don't need a rest," he said. "But your vegetables need planting. Besides, I've got to start back early tomorrow morning."

"Even if you don't want to rest, you must eat something. Aren't you hungry? Come on!"

"I won't turn down a meal," said the young man. "But first let's have a look at your vegetable plot. We can plan the sowing while we eat."

Chao-hsien nodded, thinking at the same time that here was one who knew how to make the best use of

46

time. The two went directly to the vegetable plot, talking as they hurried along.

Just then Mrs Meng arrived at the village entrance. She had come to call her daughter home for lunch. Pleasantly surprised to see her daughter with the young man, she turned into the brigade office.

Her husband and the old accountant had just returned from the fields and the accountant was fumbling for the key to open the office door. Mrs Meng hurried up to her husband, smiling, and said to him, "Come home with me, quick. Hurry!" Without waiting for his reply, Mrs Meng brushed the dust from his clothes as she went on, "Look at you, all over dust. People will laugh. But that's nothing compared with how they'll laugh at Chao-hsien and me for being bad managers."

Puzzled by all this, the old brigade leader pretended to be angry and demanded, "What's all this fuss about? What's happened?"

"Just fancy!" went on his wife. "The letter didn't come but he's come instead."

"Who's come?" asked the old brigade leader, still at a loss.

The old accountant folded his hands and chuckled, "So, it looks like we're going to have a wedding feast. It must be Chao-hsien's young man."

"Nothing of the kind! This is the first I've heard of it," said the brigade leader, shaking his head.

"If she didn't even tell her mother, of course she wouldn't have told you," his wife said impatiently. "The young man's already sitting in our house, and you're still in the dark!"

They hurried home. Chao-hsien had just fetched the guest a basin of hot water to wash up.

"Here are my father and mother. My father's the head of our production brigade," Chao-hsien told the young man. And turning to her parents she said, "This is Comrade Wang Yuan-ching from south of the river. . . ."

"Fancy meeting you for the first time today. Why don't you drop in more often?" said the girl's mother.

"This is the first time we've met too," Chao-hsien said, and went on to explain how Wang Yuan-ching had come to help them.

Her mother was a little disappointed. Then, impressed by what the young man had done, she smiled.

The brigade leader gave his wife a quizzical glance and then warmly invited the guest to join them at lunch. During the meal he expressed his gratitude to the young man and asked how things were going south of the river. But Mrs Meng managed to slip in a whole series of questions about his age, his family, and so forth. When he told her that he and his old mother lived alone, she smiled and said, "Your mother is a lucky woman, having such a progressive and able son as you." And she helped him to a second large steamed roll.

The people of Mengchiatan were very moved and encouraged by the help pouring in from all sides in the form of vegetable seed and even with the planting. That afternoon, the brigade leader assigned twenty more members to help the vegetable growers with their work.

The young man was as active on the vegetable plot as if he were in his own production brigade. He first suggested sowing by drilling or dibbling, instead of scattering the seed broadcast. The result was that the seed went twice as far and covered the entire double-size plot. This in itself impressed the villagers, especially Chao-hsien. She learned from Young Wang by watching how he worked, asking him to demonstrate his sowing method and acting as his assistant. The young man worked systematically and swiftly so that the seed was soon evenly spaced out and covered uniformly and smoothly with soil. Not only Chao-hsien, but the other commune members, too, acclaimed his skill.

Early the next morning Wang Yuan-ching took his leave. The brigade leader and the entire vegetable group accompanied him out of the village, reluctant to see him go. There was no sign of Chao-hsien's usual vivacity either, as she walked silently beside Young Wang to the river. "How can we ever thank you, Comrade Wang Yuan-ching?" But this was all she could say.

The young man looked at the girl as though seeing her for the first time. "No need to thank me. I hope you'll raise fine cabbages and turnips. That will be the best way to thank us."

Chao-hsien looked up and said firmly, "Yes, I promise we will. But I hope you'll come back in the autumn, to see our crop for yourself."

The young man took off his shoes and waded back across the river, just as he had done the day before. The girl's gaze followed him, and she waved. As she watched his receding figure, a warm feeling came over her. Besides bringing them seed and gardening knowledge, he had made a less definable but indelible impression on her, with his selfless help to another collective than his own.

Suddenly Mrs Meng came running up. "Stop him!" she shouted. "He's forgotten his seed bag."

Chao-hsien took the bag from her mother. "Don't call him," she said. "He'll come again in the autumn. And if he doesn't, I'll take it to him."

August 14, 1960

Illustration by Tung Chen-sheng

The previous summer they wanted to plant trees during the rainy season, but there was not a single sapling in the whole brigade. Mother Chu refused to ask other brigades for them, nor would she agree to buying saplings.

She led the commune members in searches for saplings in the recesses deep in the mountains, and they also collected tree seeds from everywhere. Besides planting the saplings, they opened up a piece of wasteland to set out a tree nursery as a long-term reserve.

I had hurried up the mountain, arriving at the brigade before noon. The Party branch secretary had gone to work in the nursery 5 *li* away, I was told, and I was enthusiastically greeted by a young man who was their accountant. After reading my letter of introduction he smiled and said, "We've been expecting a newspaper reporter for a long time! We'd like you to report on the work of our Party branch secretary. We're proud of what she's done."

I asked the young man where the Party branch secretary was.

"You want to talk with her?" he said. "It's no use. She'd only tell you her own shortcomings and little of what she's really done. Better talk with some team leaders and ordinary commune members. And what they forget to mention I'll fill in, for I know the story well."

Accordingly, he asked a group of young men and women to meet me.

"Say something about our tree planting," he said, "about the example our Party branch secretary has set up. Give the comrade reporter a picture of what we've done. The whole country will soon know how we've covered our bald old Taku Mountain with trees. Like the labour models Wang Kuo-fan and Li Shun-ta, our Party branch secretary will surely go to Peking and be received by Chairman Mao!"

Our talk was animated, and I learned a lot. During lunch, while the accountant was reckoning up figures for me, I went to the Party branch secretary's home to wait for her. She returned later than all the others, and when she learned I had come from Peking, she greeted me as warmly as though I were one of her own kin. I told her what my task was, and said I must go back down the mountain that day. So, instead of sitting down to have her meal, she took a piece of cornbread and munched it as she showed me all over the mountain.

"Just staying indoors and talking isn't enough," she said. "You must take a look round. What we've done is all here for you to see!"

I exclaimed over the young trees, which filled the gullies.

"We still have a long way to go," she said. "We planned to have three gullies covered in two years, but we succeeded in covering only two. Our plantings in the third were destroyed by cattle and sheep. It was my fault. I didn't know about separating the afforested area from the pasture."

Then I noticed with amazement the slopes covered with numerous new pits.

"This also should not be. The tree nursery ought to have been started right at the beginning. But I didn't think the matter through. We started the nursery only this year, and there aren't nearly enough saplings."

As we walked and talked on the way, I checked with her on the material I had been given by the others, telling her that I intended to write about the afforestation of the barren Taku Mountain.

She thought a while and then said, "I don't quite understand why you want to write about this little bit of work we've done, but if it may inspire others, then go ahead and report it as it is."

Before leaving, I asked her how she overcame so many difficulties to achieve so much. She simply said, "What we have done is far from enough. Besides, it's only what we ought to do." At the time, I did not realize the full significance of her words.

That night, in the snow and wind, my hands and feet were numb with the cold. I quickly opened up my luggage to prepare for sleep. Then suddenly came rapid knocks on the gate.

I stopped to listen. There were also loud shouts which were swept away by the wild wind.

"Comrade . . . from the press . . . open the door. . . ."

The call was obviously for me. I threw my coat over my shoulders and opened the door. There was a rush of cold wind carrying snowflakes into the room.

Wrapping my coat tightly around me, I dashed to the front gate, removed the bar and opened it. Someone was there all right, covered with snow.

A hurricane-lantern cast its light weakly in the tempest, and I could not see who the person was.

"Sorry to disturb you, comrade," the late caller apologized. Then I recognized the voice as that of Mother Chu. I was surprised. What had brought her out on such a night!

"There is a mistake in the figures we gave you today — 300 more pits than we actually did," said Mother Chu, warming her hands by blowing her breath on them. "That young man was careless. He included the 300-some pits dug in the autumn in the figure for the winter." She had some difficulty extracting a slip of paper from her pocket with her cold hands. "Take this," she said. "Here are the correct figures."

I took the slip of paper, saying, "It's so cold. Come in and warm yourself first."

But she would not. After brushing off the snow that had fallen on her head, she repeated with emphasis, "You must correct it! We've already reported the autumn figure, and to report the 300 pits again would give a false figure. That would mean 300 extra pits — and then 300 extra trees which did not exist. There would be endless errors. This must be corrected!"

"Right, I'll correct it immediately," I hastened to reply.

As if still not reassured, she said again, "The figure will be accurate after the correction. To be sure, I counted the pits again after you left. . . ."

Very moved, I said to myself, "Easy enough, it might seem, counting pits, but what a job it actually was!" I pictured in my mind this woman, no longer young, making her way over the rocks and wild grass, the biting cold wind blowing and tearing at the hem of her blue cotton jacket and her grey-streaked hair, the thorny wild date shrubs catching at her trouser-legs. She would have been oblivious to everything else, pointing with her large, calloused finger, her attention on every new mound of earth as she counted: one, two, three. . . .

Then, for still stronger emphasis, the woman said again, "Your report will appear in the Party papers. The leading comrades and the masses will read it — many people. Isn't that so?" Every word she said was clear, a reminder to me that my facts must be correct.

At a loss for words, I only kept nodding my head, feeling that indeed I was not attentive and conscientious enough in working for the Party's cause, whether my assignment was big or small. Now here was this woman, a veteran Party member, expressing her sense of responsibility to the revolution. Only now did I understand what she had said to me on parting. And the tiny slip of paper correcting an error weighed heavily on my hand, searing it a little too. My eyes moistened, and I stepped forward to grasp Mother Chu's icy hand. "You're quite right," I managed to say. "What you have done and what you say are all correct . . . . Now please come in and have a rest."

Shaking the snow from her shoulders, she replied softly but firmly, "No, I have to get back to the mountain. . . ."

"Get back to the mountain?"

"Yes, I must," Mother Chu answered. Then, turning up the flame in her lantern, she said, "When I started out, the snow wasn't so heavy. The tree nursery up the mountain may not be able to stand the storm."

"Let me go with you up the mountain."

"There's no need. I can get back up that path without any trouble. Aren't you going back tomorrow?"

"Let me see you across the river at least."

Mother Chu did not refuse that offer. I took the lantern from her hand and, lighting the way with it, we set out.

The north wind, as though making a show of its force, swept up the snow and kept flinging it in our faces till I could no longer feel the sting. I took off my overcoat and tried to put it around the woman, but she would not hear of it, and there seemed even a little anger in her voice as she ordered me to wear it myself.

The wind grew stronger outside the village, and we could inch our way forward only by exerting all our energy against it, as if we were struggling out of thick brush. Suddenly, Mother Chu stopped and called out, "Wait a minute."

I thought she had reconsidered making the trip back, and was relieved. "It really is hard going, isn't it?"

"Yes, but we have to go on. However, there's something I have to attend to in the village first."

So we turned back and, with the wind at our backs, were soon in the village. Turning down a small lane, we stopped before a wooden gate in a low wall on which Mother Chu banged forcefully with her strong palm.

"Young Wang, open the gate!" she shouted through a crack in the door. She called several times but there was no response. Then, with a faint smile, she said, "Young people sleep soundly."

She called again, more loudly, till at last there was a reply from inside. "Is it Mother Chu? Yes, yes, I'm coming." A door inside creaked, followed by a cry of surprise, "What a storm!"

57

The gate opened and a young man appeared before us, a padded jacket over his shoulders and not looking cold at all.

Walking straight into the yard, Mother Chu said, "Inspect the horse and cattle sheds at once. This snow is early and heavy. How have you prepared against it? Where are the two foals that were born on the seventh of this month?"

"In shed No. 6," the young fellow replied.

"Put them in another. That shed's too high, and there's a window at the back. It's bound to be colder than the others. The young foals won't be able to stand the cold!"

Taking over the lantern, Mother Chu inspected the sheds one by one, from the paling gate to the ceiling, from the manger to the floor, and took a look at every animal, each stretching its neck towards her, breathing out warm air, neighing and lowing. The young stockman and I followed closely behind her.

"Mother Chu, are they all right?" the young fellow asked anxiously.

"All except No. 7," Mother Chu nodded and said. "It faces west, and the northwest wind blows right into it. Get someone quickly to fetch some sorghum stalks to ward off the wind."

We left the stockbreeding yard still in the wind and snow. Mother Chu said to me, "I want to look up the store-keeper. I'm not sure the potato cellars are well covered over."

Turning north, we came to the yard where the store-keeper lived. Mother Chu stopped me when I tried to step forward to knock at the gate before she did.

Illustration by Tung Chen-sheng

She said, smiling, "The store-keeper is old and works conscientiously. We have only to call him and he'll wake and see to the cellars. No need to help him make a detailed inspection." With that she stepped onto a stone and called into the yard, "Old Store-keeper!"

Suddenly, someone spoke from behind us, "Here I am!"

Mother Chu jumped down from the stone and asked the old man approaching us, "Our potato cellars? How about them?"

"They're all right now," said the store-keeper who was now standing before us covered with snow. "We've just finished covering them over. No snow has gotten into them. The brigade leader is helping the people to cover them over with straw. I'm going to the stockbreeding yard to see how things are there."

After telling the old man about the situation in the stockbreeding yard and asking him about other matters, Mother Chu decided to return to the mountain right away. She said to the store-keeper, "Tell the brigade leader to get the people to carry all the snow on the slopes and the roads to the wheat fields as soon as it stops snowing tomorrow. Pile it thick, so that we don't have to use freezing water later."

Again, we went out of the village. The storm raged on, but by now I had forgotten about feeling cold. After crossing the Chuho River bridge, Mother Chu would not listen to my accompanying her further. "See you later," she said and, taking over the lantern, plunged into the immense whiteness of the snow.

From the bank of the Chuho River I watched the tall figure of Mother Chu with her flickering lantern light gradually disappear into the distance.

There seemed to be new fire within me, a flame capable of melting the immense snow. . . .

February 17, 1961

Bright Clouds

THE morning air was crisp and sweet. Along the street the low fence was covered with the green leaves and young tendrils of climbing beans and half-open convolvulus blossoms. As I walked past, the dewdrops beading the thick foliage were shaken onto the loose soil at the foot of the fence.

Following the directions offered by a neighbourhood child, I went on down the street looking for the team leader's house. Soon, I noticed a tall poplar on the north side with an old grindstone beneath it. This must be it.

Quietly, I entered by the half-open gate. In the yard two white geese, necks stretched, hissed angrily. A flock of speckled hens flapped their wings as they scurried from under my feet. Outside the north room, a woman was standing on a high stool papering the window. As she had her back towards me, I could not see who she was, but I imagined she must be the team leader's wife.

"Is the team leader home, sister-in-law?" I asked, coming to a standstill.

"No," she answered without turning her head or stopping her work.

"Where is he?" I took a step forward.

61

"He has two legs under him, where can't he go? I haven't tied him with ropes!" This retort, rugged as a rock, was hurled back at me.

I'd come specially to see the team leader on my first visit to Nantsun Village. When I met him in the commune office a few days back, I made an appointment to meet him here this morning.

"If I happen to be out for a while, my wife is sure to take care of you," he had assured me, giving me the impression that his wife must be a hospitable as well as capable woman, like so many wives of leading village comrades I'd met before. I didn't expect to be snubbed like this the moment I set foot in their yard, and couldn't quite make up my mind whether to stay or leave. I decided I'd better go and wait in the office of the production team. But before I could turn away, I heard her call out, "What's the matter? If you've something to say, say it." Fixing the last of the white squares of paper into the window frame, she did not even bother to look round to see who I was.

"I've come to see the team leader," I said again, a little exasperated this time.

"Ha . . . ha . . ." she laughed, startling me with her sudden outburst. Lightly, she jumped off the stool and stalked towards me.

I glanced at her in annoyance. She seemed to be around thirty and had round eyes and thin lips in a squarish face with a pointed chin. Tall and slim, she wore ordinary cotton clothes, well made, though faded from much washing. There was that special air of smartness about her peculiar to capable, strong-minded women.

"Oh!" she suddenly cried out in surprise. "I thought it was San-niu from the west end. Your voice is just like his. Comrade, where did you come from?" She appeared on the verge of laughter again but restrained herself as she eyed me curiously.

I answered her that I came from the provincial capital and wanted to see the team leader about an important matter.

She changed her casual air. "Do come in and sit down," she invited, nodding seriously by way of greeting. As I walked slowly towards the house, she turned and went in. She emerged again in the twinkling of an eye, a kettle in her left hand and a low stool over that arm while in her right arm she hugged a small table with short legs. Two tea cups were hooked on the fingers of her right hand. The table and stool were placed before me in a jiffy and I immediately smelled the fragrance of newly-brewed tea. She did everything with such efficiency that after my initial surprise I realized here was a woman who not only had a sharp tongue, but was very capable as well.

"Here, come and sit down. Have some tea. He has to go to town this morning, but he's not gone yet. He's doing a bit of work in the fields with the other members. I can tell you, it's no simple task to be a team leader — all year long and never a good night's sleep. Luckily, he has a very strong constitution because he started roughing it in the fields with his father when he was very small. Otherwise he might have collapsed long ago. Why don't you sit down? He'll be back in a moment."

As the woman talked she deftly poured me a cup of tea. When I picked up the cup to drink, she stood beside

63

me and continued her tale of the morning. Perhaps she wanted to explain the cause of her earlier rudeness or maybe she just wanted to let off steam about San-niu, whom she mistook me for. "It made me angry so early in the morning. This morning, the team leader asked me to find lodgings for a comrade from the provincial paper—"

At this point, as if she had made a sudden discovery, she smiled at me. "Oh! That reporter must be you. And I thought since San-niu had an unoccupied room which is nice and big, and they've no children, it'd be just ideal for you to do your reading and writing in without being disturbed. I went there to discuss this with his wife. I did my best to persuade her, gave her every reason I could think of . . . but that woman positively refused. What's more, she insinuated that I was intentionally making trouble for her. How terrible that woman is! Yesterday she was none too pleased when the team leader asked her to carry drinking water to comrades working in the fields. Today she intentionally picked a quarrel with me. I was extremely irritated. If not for the sake of the team leader I would have quarrelled with her. You see, comrade, since my husband became team leader, it has more or less cured my wilfulness. I have to think twice before I take a single step. For instance, it was decided that beginning yesterday, boiled water should be sent during the break to those working in the fields. The production team assigned San-niu's wife to send it, but she considered the job too troublesome and was unwilling to do it. The team leader felt this problem difficult to deal with and fixed his eyes on me so that I had to raise my hand to show my willingness to do it. As the team leader's wife I have to give way to everyone.

Illustration by Tung Chen-sheng

After filling my cup with more tea he poured himself some. Then, sipping it, he turned to his wife and said with a smile, "So you quarrelled with San-niu's wife again, eh?"

She whirled round, her anger flaring up once more. "Me quarrel with her?" she demanded. "As if I had the time and energy."

"Never mind who quarrelled with whom. You should first examine yourself and see whether you were in the right," said her husband.

"So, what's this?" she cried. "It's your turn to say who's in the right this time. Listen, I'll start from the beginning. . . ."

"Never mind," said the team leader, waving his hand. "You needn't say any more, I know all about it."

She flushed. "D'you mean you won't let me speak? Is this a democratic style of work for a team leader?"

"All right, all right. If you like I won't do anything all afternoon but just sit at home listening to you. Will that do?" Actually he was very proud of his wife, and he turned to me to explain. "This happens with us all the time." After another sip of tea, he asked his wife, "Has anyone come asking for me?"

She turned her head away on purpose, answering crossly, "Of course. The carters were looking for you again. They want you to get a move on and buy them some new horse collars."

"Ho, buy this, buy that!" He was serious now. Pointing to the old collars, he said, "The collars cost more than four yuan each. If these are patched and mended they'll do instead of buying new ones. That'll save us twenty yuan at least."

"Go ahead and mend them then. Don't leave them around here."

The team leader's black eyes twinkled. "I must find some skilful person to mend them," he said.

She snorted and stamped into the house.

The team leader exchanged a few more casual words with me before he observed that the sun was getting high in the sky, and stood up to leave. His wife dashed out to call him back. "Weren't you going to find someone to mend these collars? Why leave them here? They're dirty and smelly. I'll throw them in the ditch if you don't take them away."

"Oh, yes, talking to Comrade Liang, I clean forgot about them. And we'll need them when the carts go out this afternoon." The team leader affectedly tapped his forehead and turned to his wife with a smile. "I say, d'you think you could help out?"

She cocked her head. "I'm not good at mending. Besides, it's none of my business."

"How difficult it is to ask a favour! All right, it's none of your business." So saying, he headed for the door.

She rushed out to stop him. "What kind of a team leader are you? Even if this is a work assignment, you ought to ask me politely."

He laughed. "Polite words are easy. Listen, comrade, will you please do it, for my sake and. . . ."

She chuckled, then stretching out her hand, she said, "Give me some cloth to patch them with. Am I to mend them with air?"

"Cloth? Oh, I forgot. Well, we haven't any in the office. I'll tell you what. Use some of yours. The team will replace it some time in the future."

"Replace it? When have you ever replaced anything of mine that the team used? Take them away. I told you it's none of my business."

"Look," the team leader suddenly cried out. "The chickens are running wild all over the kitchen stove."

Both she and I turned to look at the stove, but there was not a chicken on it. When we looked back the team leader was disappearing out of the gate. I roared with laughter.

"You wretch," said she, pretending anger but laughing in spite of herself. "He's tight-fisted, that's the trouble. Won't let anyone take a cent out of the team's account."

She took me into the house. I saw that she had the room nicely cleaned for me. There was not a speck of dust anywhere. A few of the team leader's awards were hung on the walls, and a picture taken of him and other model workers and peasants at the county congress. There were also two coloured film posters which have now replaced the old-fashioned New Year pictures as wall decorations in many peasant houses. The room was not very big, but it was bright and roomy enough.

She brought the low table inside, placing it on my *kang*. "Now you can settle down to your work. If there's anything you want, just call me."

I had taken a liking to my warm-hearted, outspoken hostess. "Sister-in-law," I said, "what's your name?"

"My family name is Li," she replied, "and my own name is Bright Clouds."

"What a pretty name."

"Pretty? The team leader gave me that name the year our people's commune was founded. I asked him why I should have such an attractive name when I'm such a rough and ready person. But he insisted." She smiled. I could see she liked the name all right.

"Are you a leader of some group in the team too?"

"Do I look like one? No, I'm not." She quickly added, "Whether you're a leading comrade or not you can serve the people just as well. Since he works for the collective day in and day out, summer or winter, I feel I'm serving the people if I help him so that he has more time to do his work better. Don't you think so?"

Before I had time to reply, there was the sound of hurried footsteps in the yard.

"Is the team leader home?" It was a man's husky voice calling.

"No, he isn't," she answered.

"Doesn't matter if he isn't. I want to speak to you."

"Speak then," said Bright Clouds, going out to meet the visitor.

"There's that plot of millet on the western slope. I don't know whether it should be hoed or not. Yesterday evening when work was assigned for today, nobody mentioned it."

"That millet's on the west side. It belongs to your sector. Do you think it needs hoeing?"

"Without rain, it would have been all right to leave a few more days. But it sprinkled a little last night. That soil's no good. One day's hot sun will make it as hard as a rock. Then hoeing will be difficult."

"You ought to get a few members to hoe it then. Do it while the ground's still nice and soft." Bright Clouds spoke loudly, betraying her anxiety.

quite well that the old collars are in bad shape but he doesn't want to spend money on new ones. I don't know where he dug these out this morning, but he brought them here, all smelly and dirty. When I asked him what they were for, he said he wanted someone skilful to mend them. . . ."

"He meant you."

"I'm no fool. Don't I know it! I thought that since he wanted me to do something, he couldn't just expect me to understand unless he asked me nicely. He can go ahead and suggest all he likes. I'll just pretend to be dumb. I've quit stretching out my hand to do things. It never gets me anywhere. If it's well done I don't hear a word of praise, but if something goes wrong, he criticizes me severely. So why should I do this? It's none of my business and I'll certainly not bother."

The old woman was laughing heartily. "Oh, Bright Clouds, you may cry out, 'It's none of my business!' but what, if I may ask, are you doing right now?"

"That's why I said his tactics are terrible. He knows me inside out," said Bright Clouds, laughing too. "Tell me, do you think it's possible for me not to bother? If the animals have no collars when the carts go out, what will happen? Why, the horses will be rubbed raw, and that'll be bad for our team's work."

They laughed together loud and heartily.

When at last they stopped, Bright Clouds said, "Anyway, this is the very last time. In the future, I'm not going to bother about anything, no matter how important it is. I'll let him know I'm not to be trifled with."

72

"I came here with something really important to ask the team leader," said the old woman. "But I can see your heart is set on not bothering, so it's no use telling you about it. I'll just have to wait till the team leader gets back. Of course this'll mean holding up important business. But what can one do? The team leader's not at home."

"Don't go yet. Tell me, is it urgent?"

"Oh, rather."

"Well, tell me what it is then."

"You're not going to bother any more, so what's the use?"

"So you've also learned how to torment me. If it weren't for not wanting you to hold up any important business, I wouldn't ask you at all. I'd show you the gate. Tell me, what is it?"

After another laugh, the old woman said seriously, "Haven't you heard already? Yu-wang's wife at the east end was taken ill suddenly and had to be rushed to the hospital early this morning. . . ."

"Oh, that. I knew about it before you did. I was the one who helped to find men to carry the stretcher this morning."

"But just now the hospital sent word saying that she'll have to be there for at least a week. She's nursing a baby too, you know. What shall we do?"

"Oh, yes, we'll have to think about arrangements for her baby." Bright Clouds said this under her breath. After a few seconds, I heard her get up from her stool as she said, "Let's go and see how things are. We'll have to consult with the neighbours."

Bright Clouds did a few more things in the yard before she came to my door. "Comrade, please stay here for a while. I have to go out on some business. I'll be back soon. If anyone comes looking for the team leader, ask him to wait for me." She left with the old woman, the sound of their laughing voices drifting back to my ears.

The bright sunshine cast a fine leafy pattern of the pomegranate tree across my window-panes. Golden shafts crept into my room from the doorway. It must be nearly noon.

Bright Clouds came back flushed and perspiring. But she seemed to be extremely happy. Bustling in and out of the house, she fed the chickens, shooed away the geese, brought kindling and lit the fire in the stove. In between, a few visitors came looking for the team leader. Evidently she was too busy now to chat with them and ɛad gave them terse, precise instructions before dis-ɩssing them.

When I went out to the other room she was busy cooking. But when the fire was burning well, she sat by the stove sewing away at great speed on the collars. Finally she bit off the thread, looked up smiling, and rushed off with the whole lot in her arms.

I went out in the yard for a stroll. The team leader came home.

"Well, Comrade Liang, have you settled down in your lodging?" he asked, smiling, one hand wiping the sweat from his brow.

"Sister-in-law was very kind. She helped me arrange everything nicely."

"Yes, she's much better at this sort of thing than I," he said. "Her only trouble is a sharp tongue and quick temper. But if you know her better and understand her temperament, you find that these are actually one of her strong points. We've been married more than ten years. We never quarrel over family matters."

Just then Bright Clouds came back carrying a baby. It was a bright cute little thing, and she was obviously fond of it.

As the team leader took the baby from his wife's arms, he cooed to it, "Have you been fed yet, my little one? Come, let's have a kiss."

Bright Clouds deftly laid the table. Lunch was ready.

The team leader asked some questions about various things in the village, all of which she answered without a moment's hesitation. "Yu-wang's wife was taken to hospital this morning. I wonder how she's doing. Is there any news from the hospital yet?" he finally asked.

Bright Clouds laughed. "You ask about everything else. Why don't you ask about your precious collars?"

"I suppose you've thrown them into the ditch, so why ask about them?" answered her husband with a grin. "Really, I should find time to go to the hospital this evening to see how Yu-wang's wife is getting along. Perhaps you'd help me by going in my place to find out how she is?"

"The hospital has sent word already, she's to stay at least a week."

The team leader cuddled the baby in his arms. "Then what about this little one?" he asked. "He can't go to the hospital with her, can he?"

Bright Clouds was very smug now. "You're way behind things, comrade. We've arranged everything.

We women in the team will take turns watching and
feeding him, beginning with me on duty today. . . ."

I stared at the smiling baby in the team leader's arms.
So this wasn't their own Little Yao, the child my hostess
had been telling me about that morning.

November 1961

Rain in
Apricot Blossom Village

THE rain and the darkness interwove in a vast net that overspread hill and village. All living things had quietly sought shelter. The only sound was that of the rain and the rumbling, rolling thunder.

Leading a grey horse along the muddy road, Sung Chun-lin could hardly breathe as he struggled forward into the lashing storm. He took off his shirt and put it over the horse's back. Then he removed his undershirt and wrapped a small packet of medicine in it. Tugging the halter rope, he urged the animal on with shouts, his eyes straining to pierce the darkness.

Like many boys who have just finished school, Chun-lin had never encountered any real difficulties before. His apprehension was tempered with wishful thinking. If only the wind would blow harder, he thought, and drive the storm away. Or, better still, maybe he'd find a big building ahead where they could get out of the rain and obtain food for man and beast. He couldn't stop such wild flights of fancy as he moved with great effort along the road. But then fear again predominated, and he was consumed with despondency and regret.

77

The heat had been unusually fierce that noon. The crops drooped, the wild flowers closed their eyes. Even the stones on the hill slopes radiated the intense heat. Since Chun-lin had been at school for several years, the team leader was afraid he had grown unaccustomed to working in the hot sun and sent him home early. As Chun-lin was washing his face with cold water beneath the gourd arbour, his father came home, quite upset. He said the big grey horse was very sick, that the brigade's stableman was taking the animal into town to see the veterinarian.

Chun-lin hastily dried his face and rushed off. He caught up with the old stableman on the south ridge. "It's terribly hot and you've got a bad leg," he said. "I'll take the grey horse to the vet for you."

At first the old man wouldn't agree. He said he was responsible for the brigade's animals. But after Chun-lin gave him a dozen different guarantees, he finally consented. The boy led the horse fifteen *li* into town, had it examined, bought the medicine prescribed, and got caught in the rain on the way back. It was now completely dark. There were no villages around, not even a big tree to take shelter under. The horse had been ill a whole day. It would get worse if Chun-lin couldn't get it out of the rain soon. And how was he to face people at home if it should die?

Clambering up a low ridge, he realized that he hadn't the slightest idea where he was and his heart beat wildly. He halted and stared into the dark night with rain-misted eyes. Suddenly, he made out the glimmer of a lamp, and this lighted his heart too. Bracing himself, he pulled the horse along.

78

The rain formed many small rivulets that swirled about Chun-lin's feet. As he trudged across a number of mounds, he could see the vague outline of a grove. Chun-lin caught intermittent glimpses of the lamplight through the trees. Feeling his way, he finally reached the entrance to a small compound. The gate, blown down by the wind, lay in the mud.

A flash of lightning revealed a low one-storey house and a thatched stable standing before it. Chun-lin quickly led the horse into the stable and tied it to a post. Wiping the rain from his face, he stretched his stiff legs and heaved a sigh of relief. Only now did he realize how cold, tired and hungry he was.

Holding the medicine wrapped in his wet undershirt, Chun-lin groped through the darkness to the house. The door was shut tight. He pounded on it, shouting, "Comrade, say, comrade. . . ."

His high-pitched voice was blown away by the wind, so that the door was opened only after a long wait. He stepped inside.

"What village is this, comrade?"

The flame danced uneasily in the hurricane-lamp which his host held. After a cautious look at Chun-lin, the holder of the lamp replied, "West Apricot Blossom."

Chun-lin was startled. "How did I get all the way over here?" he exclaimed.

It was then that he saw standing before him a young woman in her twenties. She had evidently also been out in the rain and had just changed her wet clothes. Drops were still falling from her jet-black hair and her pretty face. Chun-lin noticed a big "Double Happiness" character written on a piece of red paper, pasted on the door. The freshness of its colour indicated that a wedding had taken place here very recently. Chun-lin looked around the room. The woman seemed to be alone.

Embarrassed, Chun-lin said, "Excuse me. I didn't mean to disturb you." He hurried back to the stable and untied the halter rope. But the sick horse planted its four legs squarely and stubbornly refused to budge.

"You've brought a horse? Does it belong to your brigade?" asked the young woman. She stood under the eaves still, with the lamp in her hand, the rain pouring off the roof obscuring her features like a bead curtain.

"He's sick. I've just had him to the vet. We got caught in the rain and missed the road," replied Chun-lin, pulling desperately on the rope.

"What are you doing? He'll get worse if you take him out in the rain," cried the young woman. Oblivious of the fact that she had just put on dry clothes, she ran out and immediately was soaked again.

"Is this the east end of the village or the west? If you'll give me my directions, I'll find shelter somewhere else."

"We've a stable for the horse and a place for you too. No household in the village is more convenient than ours. Besides, we're quite far from the village proper. The road is hard going," the young woman said earnestly in a voice that would brook no denial. Taking the rope from the boy's hand, she retied it to the post.

Chun-lin couldn't very well refuse. It was true — where else could he go? Moved by the woman's kindness, he said thankfully. "All right. You go back to the house. I'll stay here in the stable."

The young woman laughed. "When you come to the West Apricot Blossom, you're a guest. Who ever heard of a guest staying in the stable?"

Chun-lin could only smile awkwardly.

Cheerfully raising the lamp, the woman examined the horse from head to tail, then checked the halter rope to make sure it was fast.

"Come on in," she said. "It's cold outside."

2

The woman lit some dried corn cobs in a brazier. Little tongues of flame began to leap gaily, and the room at once seemed warm and comfortable.

Chun-lin didn't think it proper to walk around stripped to the waist and put on his wet jacket when he entered the room. He put the undershirt in which the medicine had been wrapped by the fire to dry it out. It was a yellow vest, emblazoned in red letters with "No. 2 Middle School." Chun-lin gazed with cautious curiosity about the small room.

It was bright and clean, the walls newly whitewashed. At the centre of the north wall hung a picture of Chairman Mao, flanked by vertical red scrolls inscribed with a couplet in large characters. At the foot of the east wall stood a low, red, rectangular chest, and on the wall above that, in a large picture frame, were snapshots of various sizes. Beside this, in another frame, was a citation of merit. What caught Chun-lin's eye most were the novels piled on the chest. Everything in the room at once won the boy's admiration.

"Where's the rest of your family, comrade?" he asked her.

The young woman was kneading flour, so as to make her guest something to eat.

"They're out. My father-in-law is Party secretary, my husband is deputy brigade leader. When the rain started, the three of us went to the village to see if any of our commune members' houses were leaking. One covered the east end, the other the west. I checked the section around here. Because I was nearer home, I got back first."

"What's your name?" asked Chun-lin.

"My husband's family name is Chia, my own family is called Hu. We've only been married four days. My parents live in the East Apricot Blossom." The bride put the bowl with the kneaded dough on the chest, beside the books.

"I've been there," Chun-lin said, turning his undershirt around to expose the other side to the heat.

"Maybe you know my father. Our family have been millers there for generations." The young woman placed an oblong pastry board on the table.

"Isn't your father the miller named Hu?" the boy queried animatedly, his shyness instantly vanishing. He remembered the first time he had been to the East Apricot Blossom. It was in a time of famine before the liberation, and his mother had taken him down from the hills to beg in the village streets. They had rested outside the mill at noon. Hungry and thirsty, Chun-lin had lain exhausted in the shade of a tree. The kindly miller had given him a drink of water and a ball of cooked bran. Only then did Chun-lin have the strength to go on.

The boy was still moved at the recollection. He glanced at the bride's face and said, "The year of the big famine I rested outside your gate. I saw you. You were a little girl in pigtails then. Do you remember?"

With an apologetic smile, the young woman shook her head. "We saw so many famine refugees in those days. I could never remember them all."

"After liberation, I went to school in the town. I used to pass your door on the way home for summer and winter vacations. Last June I went into your yard to ask for a drink of water. Your family's mill is part of the commune now. You've got a diesel engine and an automatic grain grinder, haven't you?"

This time the young woman nodded and smiled.

Outside, the rain was still splashing down. Suddenly, a voice called, "Hsiu-chih, where did that horse come from?"

The young woman put down her rolling pin and shouted, "Come inside, pa. We have a guest."

Outside, her father-in-law stamped his feet under the eaves. "Guests calling in weather like this?" he asked. A tall man in his fifties entered. He had a dripping oilcloth over his shoulders. His trouser legs were rolled up and his bare feet were spattered with mud. A pair of kindly eyes, flashing from a network of wrinkles, looked Chun-lin over. The boy was conscious of the friendly warmth of his gaze.

Removing the oilcloth and shaking the drops from his hands, the man took out a pouch of tobacco and began filling his pipe.

"Where are you from, young fellow?" he asked Chun-lin with a smile.

The bride spoke up before Chun-lin could answer. "He's from the Vine Gorge. His brigade's grey horse is sick. He took it into town for an examination and got caught in the rain on the way back."

"That horse is sick? And it's been out in the rain?" The father-in-law was obviously alarmed. His hands shook so that half the tobacco he had placed in the pipe fell to the ground. Casting the pouch aside, he again draped the oilcloth over his shoulders, took the lamp from the red chest, turned up the wick, and strode from the room.

Dazed by the sudden change in the man, Chun-lin, together with the bride, hurried after him.

The old man went into the thatched stable, held the lamp high and examined the horse carefully, feeling it gently in several places. Next he opened the animal's closed eyelids, and lifted its upper lip. He stood for a moment in shocked silence, then returned to the house.

"Have you done anything for it?" he asked Chun-lin.

"Not yet."

"You haven't bought the medicine?"

"Oh, I bought it all right." Chun-lin picked up the packet from the red chest. "It's here."

The old man took it from him and looked at Chun-lin sternly. "With a horse as sick as that, why haven't you dosed it if you've got the medicine?"

"Well . . . well, there wasn't time," the boy stammered.

"But you had time to dry your clothes and chew the rag?" the host said with a frown. "Is that any way for a stableman to behave?"

Reddening, Chun-lin hung his head.

Illustration by Chen Yu-hsien

The young woman glanced at him apologetically and quickly explained, "He's doing this to help the stableman, pa. He's not one himself. He's only just started learning farm work. He has no experience."

The old man turned to his daughter-in-law. "Maybe he hasn't, but you have. You hung around the mill ever since you were a child. You've had plenty to do with animals."

This time it was the young woman who blushed. "I thought I'd first get our guest something to eat," she mumbled, "then —"

"Which is more important?" the old man interrupted. "To feed somebody, or treat a sick animal?" His angry eyes indicated the two embarrassed young people. Then, in a softer tone, he said, "Draught animals are the pillars of production and construction in our mountain region. Young people don't yet understand their importance. I know your situation in the Vine Gorge very well. Before liberation the only furry animals you had over there were field rats. It wasn't till after land reform that you got a couple of long-haired donkeys. You didn't have mules and horses until your people's commune was formed. Your people have had a really tough struggle. It doesn't take much to let a horse die of illness, but just try raising one from a colt!"

The young people looked at one another, then again hung their heads. Chun-lin really felt very sorry. His nose tingled and he felt like weeping.

"Snap out of it," the man said. "Brew up the medicine. I'll help you dose the animal."

Thunder rolled, lightning flashed, the rain was falling even more heavily. From time to time they could hear the roar of the river, which was swollen with mountain torrents.

The fire in the brazier blazed brightly. After a battle, the three of them managed to get the medicine down the horse's throat, and now, feeling easier, they returned to the house.

The old man washed his hands and looked at Chun-lin in a more kindly manner. Filling his pipe, he said to his daughter-in-law with a smile, "Now you can get our guest something to eat. How about a bowl of hot soup and noodles with a bit of ginger? That'll warm him up and make him perspire. People who aren't used to being out in the rain get sick easily when they're soaked."

The young woman added some corn cobs to the fire. She smiled an innocent smile and started for the kitchen with the dough.

"Wait a minute," said her father-in-law. "First give him some dry clothes. It's uncomfortable to walk around dripping wet." To Chun-lin he said, "After you've eaten, you can rest in my room. There's a bed and a quilt waiting for you. The chances are eight out of ten your horse will get well after that medication. But don't forget to walk it as soon as the rain stops, the longer the better."

"Are you going out again, pa?" the young woman asked.

"Yes. The rain is still coming down hard. I'd better have a look at the new dam. It may have been weakened by such pelting rain."

"Haven't people gone already?"

"I won't feel right till I see for myself." The old man threw the oilcloth over his shoulders, smiled and nodded goodbye at Chun-lin, then went out again into the storm.

Chun-lin and the young woman accompanied him with the lamp to the gate. A flash of lightning revealed him striding off, then he disappeared in the darkness. For some reason the sight brought a rush of warmth to Chun-lin, and tears to his eyes.

3

After stopping in the thatched shed for a look at the sick grey horse, Chun-lin returned dejectedly to the house and lay down on the old man's bed. He wanted the rain to stop immediately and the sky to clear, so that he could walk the horse. But the storm continued unabated as if to spite him.

The old man's room was different from the new couple's. Here everything was very simple. On an old-fashioned table stood a pewter lamp, a stack of account books, a pair of spectacles and two blue and white vases, in one of which was stuck a feather duster. By the table stood a wooden bench. A few big white gourds lay on the floor. The flame in the pewter lamp kept leaping, like Chun-lin's thoughts.

In fact, he was very tired. His whole body seemed disjointed and his legs ached painfully. With an effort, he leaned over and blew out the lamp, then stretched out. Gradually the noise of the thunderstorm faded out and he dozed off, only to be awakened suddenly by the voice of the young woman in the next room.

"Where have you been, that you've come back so late? Has something gone wrong with one of those houses?" she was demanding loudly.

"They're sturdy as apartment buildings," a young man replied hoarsely, his reply accompanied by the sound of wringing out water. "They're in good shape."

"Oh, that's fine."

"But I'm freezing. What have you got to warm me up?"

"Quiet! We have a guest in the house," the young woman said to her husband.

"A guest? From the commune office?"

"From the Vine Gorge Commune. He got caught in the rain. Hurry and wash up and come to sleep."

"I can't. Get the fire going and make some wheat-cakes. The more the better."

"Are you crazy?"

"I'm not, but the weather is. All this rain and the mountain torrents have washed the bridge out. There's a bus cut off on the other side of the river."

The young woman uttered a little cry.

Chun-lin, awake on the old man's bed, was shocked. He had a grandmother living by the river. He used to visit her as a child and he knew the river's disposition well. In good weather it was clear and placid; in shallow places you could wade across. But in the rainy season it turned into a muddy torrent, deep and turbulent and exceedingly swift. For ten *li* on the other side there was nothing but dunes. When the heavy rains came, the dunes were separated from one another by innumerable rapid streams. The bus from the county town was probably marooned on one of them. There would be old and young passengers in it, cut off from anywhere. They would be suffering. . . .

"The passengers are pretty hungry. Some of the kids are crying," the young man's voice said heavily.

"How do you know? Has one of the passengers swum over?"

"They don't know this river. Who would risk it? I went down to the bend to see if our millet crop was flooded, and I noticed a flash on the other side. At first I thought it was lightning. But it didn't look like lightning. Then I heard them blowing their horn, so I knew it was the bus. I ran to the bridge, but it had been washed away by the torrent. All I could do was shout across the water. I nearly yelled myself hoarse before they finally heard me." Then, to his bride, the young man said, "Better start making those wheatcakes. The brigade leader is going from door to door right now collecting food. We can give our wheatcakes to the old folks and the youngsters."

"This wretched weather. How hungry and cold they must be. I'll knead some dough, you get the fire going. There are stalks out in the stable. Be careful the horse doesn't kick you."

"What horse?"

"I told you we have a guest."

"Aha, a general on horseback."

The young woman laughed. "Don't be funny."

Chun-lin could hear a pan being scraped, water being ladled, the board bumping against a vat as the young woman rolled out the dough. Then stalks began crackling in the stove, while in the background the young husband and wife conversed in warm low tones.

Chun-lin forgot his own troubles as he heard about the stranded people. He simply couldn't lie there any longer. He wanted to go out and talk to the young couple.

"Will they send someone to pick up the food when it's ready?" asked the young woman.

"Who could they send? Put it in a hamper and I'll swim across with it," the young man replied firmly.

The young woman uttered a little cry.

"What's the matter?" asked her husband.

"I burned my hand. Don't stuff so many stalks into the stove. You're scorching the wheatcakes." Her voice shook a little.

A silence followed. Even the kindling seemed to stop crackling.

After a long while the young woman spoke again. "The river's so swollen and the night's so dark. Must you go alone? It's too dangerous."

"Well, what do you suggest? That I don't go at all? Can I just stand by and watch those people over there suffer?"

"I don't mean you shouldn't go. But try and find a few more men to go with you."

"Who? The fellows who know how to swim are all up at the dam. Even our sick brigade leader is out collecting food — hobbling around with a cane."

There was another silence.

"I'll go with you," the young woman said.

The husband startled. "But you can't swim."

"I know. But I can watch you cross. That will be better than worrying at home. Anyhow, it will give you courage."

"No need for you to go out in this rain again," the husband said tenderly. "You just wait for me at home. There's no danger. I'm a good swimmer. . . ."

"It doesn't matter what you say. I'm going along."

Chun-lin sat up, bounded out of bed, and rushed into the next room.

It was warm and smoky in there. Squatting beside the young woman was a powerfully built young man whose big hands were feeding dried stalks into the stove. On the rolling board was a stack of hot wheatcakes that gave off a delightful odour.

"I'll go with you," said Chun-lin in a low but forceful tone.

The surprised husband and wife turned to look at him. It was obvious they hadn't heard what he had said.

The young man gave him a friendly if somewhat mischievous grin. "Not asleep yet, comrade?" he asked.

Chun-lin gazed at his host. He was half a head taller than himself and much stronger. His handsome weather-beaten face glowed in the firelight with youthful vitality. His eyes had the same determined, kindly cast as those of his father, the Party secretary.

"I'll go with you to take the food across the river, comrade," Chun-lin announced firmly.

The young man rose swiftly and looked Chun-lin over and asked, "Can you swim well? That water is deep and fast."

"Sure," Chun-lin nodded. "My grandmother lives by the river. I learned to swim there. I'm not afraid of the roughest water. I can help you get across."

A freshly made wheatcake in her hand, the young woman was staring at the two of them. The doubtful expression left her face when she heard Chun-lin say he was a good swimmer, but to be sure, she asked, "Are you really a strong swimmer, comrade? This is no joke."

The husband smiled and clapped Chun-lin on the shoulder. "Fine," he said. "We'll go together."

4

The storm seemed to tire. The rain stopped, and then started and stopped again. In the room the flame in the kerosene lamp leaped fitfully. . . .

The two men returned with empty food hampers, talking and laughing loudly as they walked, paying no attention to the wind and rain. It was as if they were coming home leisurely at sunset after their usual day's work in the fields, breathing the cool evening air. Entering the compound over the gate which the wind had blown down, they went, as if by agreement, to the thatched stable.

Chun-lin got there first. He felt around in the darkness, then asked in an alarmed voice, "What could have happened to the grey horse? It's gone!"

"Impossible." The young husband also came in and groped for the animal. He emerged quickly and shouted towards the house, "Hsiu-chih, Hsiu-chih, wake up. Is this how you look after the horse?"

He called several times. The sound of the rain was the only response.

The young fellows hurried into the house together. Chun-lin waited in the outer room while the other ran into the bedroom. When he turned up the wick of the hurricane-lamp, which had burned down, he saw there was no one in the room. The embers in the brazier had long since turned cold. Quite upset, the young husband came rushing out.

"That's strange," he said to Chun-lin. "She's not home."

"The horse must have got loose and run away," surmised Chun-lin, "and she's gone after it."

"Come on, we'll look too. Don't worry. In this storm, it won't run very far."

Carrying the lamp, the two young fellows searched in front of the compound and behind it, down the street, around the outskirts of the village. But not a trace of the young woman or the animal could they find. They began to worry. Then, at the north end of the village, they heard a tapping sound in the mill.

"What's that?" asked the young husband.

"A horse's hoofs," cried Chun-lin.

The two raced for the mill, the young man in the lead, holding the lamp high. There in the mill was the bride of four days, hands behind her back, leading the grey horse by the halter rope round and round the millstone.

"Haha," exclaimed her husband happily. "So this is where you do your exercises."

The scene gave Chun-lin a renewed feeling of warmth as he stood silent in the doorway of the mill out of the rain.

February 1962

93

Honeymoon

A VISITOR in Tientsin, I am quite at leisure after supper. By way of a walk, I saunter to the bank of the Haiho River.

Dusk gives the river a different look. In the haze, the steel bridge and storeyed buildings loom dimly, and the ripples give out a pale glimmer. A damp breeze, cool and refreshing, blows away the day's stuffiness.

More and more people are coming to the riverside. But this does not make the place any noisier. The old folks sit quietly in the brighter sections of the bank, sipping their tea and wielding a fan. Young couples, of whom there are a great many, either lean silently on the railing along the river, or sit on the benches talking softly to each other. In the quiet and calm of the evening, one feels the throb of a happy life.

I stroll on, feasting my eyes on the summer evening scene. Suddenly, a voice calls out to me, "Old Liang, what luck to bump into you here!" Then the owner of the voice appears from behind a flowering shrub and throws his powerful arms tightly around my shoulders. In the pale light, I cannot see clearly what he looks like, but he seems to have the vigour of youth.

"Why stare at me so! Don't you recognize me? I'm. . . ."

I remember him now. "Why, you're Young Pine! Who'd expect to meet you here!"

He smiles openly, shaking my shoulders all the while. Has he something to tell me, but doesn't know how?

"You still work in Chihsien County, don't you? How is your family? Is your —?"

"You ask about my family?" Now he begins to talk, his words pouring out in a rapid stream. "Hi, a great change has taken place in our parts. The year before last we extended a river to our village. Though not quite as big as the Haiho, it provides enough water for cooking, and the fields besides. We're sure to have a good harvest this year. . . ."

I pull him to a bench, which stands in front of a bush I do not know the name of. It has luxuriant leaves and garlands of blossom. The colour of the blossom is difficult to tell in the dusk, but I am aware of a delicate fragrance.

All of a sudden, the Young Pine of three years ago comes back to my mind.

That year, too, I was in Tientsin for work, and was living in a guest house in a quiet residential area. One day in the courtyard, I saw a group of teen-agers arguing with the old gate-keeper.

"Why are you so hard on us? We'll get in anyway, whatever you say." Standing at the head of the boys and girls was a lanky young man. He had a head of touselled hair and was slightly snub-nosed. He wore a white short-sleeved shirt, shorts and rubber shoes. His shoulders thrown back, he was glaring and shouting at the old man.

"You can come in all right, but you must make clear who you want to see!" The old man, barring the way with outstretched arms, was obviously trying hard to suppress his irritation.

"We want to see some cadre from the countryside!"

"But *all* the guests here are from the countryside!"

"We want someone from the mountains, the high mountains," said the young man with the snub nose, jerking his head.

"What's his name? Fill in a visitor's card."

The young man was caught. Looking back at his group, he put out his tongue in a grimace, after which he began to plead with the gate-keeper. "Well, please get us someone — anyone you see fit."

The old man's patience was at an end and, pushing them outside the gate, he shouted, "You trouble-makers, go and play somewhere else."

This was too good a chance to miss. The snub-nosed youth shouted at the top of his lungs, "He's swearing at us, comrades. Let's charge, comrades. Charge!"

At the shout, the youngsters poured into the courtyard, laughing uproariously.

Some of them spotted me. A girl said to the others in an undertone, "Look here, that comrade over there seems to be from the countryside." The young man shot a glance at me and grinned. He came up to me in one stride, made a deep bow and said bluntly, "Comrade, are you from the countryside? Would you do us a favour?" Pointing to the youngsters around him, he continued, "We'll graduate from middle school shortly.

Our classmates have talked it over and decided we are all going to do big things for the state. Some will continue with their study, going to engineering or agricultural colleges. Some choose to go to factories or farm machinery plants. These comrades here and I have made up our minds to go to the countryside. The school authorities say they will try and send us to the suburbs. But we feel the suburbs are too near — not challenging enough. We want to go to the mountains, to the most difficult places. Will you please find somewhere for us? My name is Young Pine. His name is. . . ."

Young Pine — the name fitted him perfectly. In fact all the youngsters before me were like growing young pines.

That was our first meeting. Then for several days he would come to my room with his friends, telling me their ideals and asking for my help. They were enthusiastic and in real earnest. Once he even brought his father with him to show how determined he was. The father was a veteran lathe turner with twenty-five years of experience behind him. Simple and quiet, he was very different from his son. He told me that Young Pine was almost eighteen and should travel his own road now. With the Party pointing the way, he couldn't go wrong. He only wanted to remind him that once one chooses his work, he should stick to it, that he did not like novelty-seekers.

Later, I went to their school. The authorities supported their idea too. Duty-bound, I promised to give my help and wrote to an old friend of mine in Panshan, a district in the old liberated area. In a few days, the district authorities contacted the school, welcoming the students to settle down there. Not long afterwards, Young Pine and his classmates graduated from the school and became the new, educated peasants in the Hsiangkuoyu Production Brigade, Panshan District, Chihsien County of Hopei Province.

Now, three years have passed. Quite unexpectedly I have met him again here. He has grown tall and sturdy. His hand is like a band of iron on my arm.

"You've never left Panshan, have you?"

"No. Last year, I was admitted into the Party. In spring, the members of our production team elected me their deputy leader. I said I wasn't good enough. But they insisted," he says, laughing.

"You don't say! Why, the Young Pine has grown into a big timber tree!"

"Not at all. I'm still scrub. But I've taken root in the countryside. Really, I have." He repeats this a second time, unable to contain his pride.

The street lights along the eastern bank are bright now without our knowing when they were turned on. Thousands of golden rays reflect on the water and quiver perpetually. Boats of all sizes coming back from afar are lowering their sails by the shore for the night. The hum of casting anchors and rushing about is carried to our ears. After a while it subsides and all becomes quiet again.

Both of us seem to have a lot to say, but don't know where to begin. Young Pine, laughing, repeats once again that he has taken root in the countryside. I begin to suspect that he has something to say to me. Sure enough, tightly grasping my shoulder, he bashfully tells me in a low voice, "Old Liang, I've got married, just a week ago."

98

"So, you've come back for your honeymoon?"

"That's right. Do you know Sunflower?"

"What, Sunflower's your wife?" I cannot help exclaiming.

He nods with a smile.

In my mind's eye, I see a vigorous girl running to me laughing. She is just like a sunflower in a mountain village. I came to know her shortly before I met Young Pine. She was a production team leader, very capable and straightforward. Many young men in the village were attracted to her, but they were a little afraid of her at the same time. It was said that she had a distant relative in Peking who was very fond of her and often bought her things, trying to induce her to the city and a life of ease. Once he gave her a jersey, a pair of woolen slacks and accessories, and insisted that she doll herself up and go to the city with him. She was furious. Looking her sternest, she said to him, "We mountain people long for a happy life even in our dreams. But we don't want your favours! You'd better forget the whole thing. If you come again with this nonsense of yours, I'll drive you out with the broom!" This had become the talk of the village for some time.

I cannot help laughing when I recall this story.

"Why do you laugh?" says Young Pine. "Isn't it true that we have taken root in the countryside? Maybe you think she is rather sharp and I'm little less so, and we make a fine couple? Well, it's quite true." He leans back on the bench and thinks for a while with eyes closed. Then he resumes his talk animatedly.

"At our wedding, my schoolmates and friends asked me to tell my love story. But I simply could not find anything to say. Our love seemed to have sprung from constant contending. There you go, laughing again! Listen to me!

"Three years ago, I made up my mind to go to the countryside. My ambition was to do something big, to perform some feats like a hero. You know all about it. Looking back, I feel it was a bit childish. But then my determination rested entirely on this ambition. In my school days, I often read *People's Daily* to look for 'big things.' It is the organ of the Party Central Committee. Whatever it approves is undoubtedly a big thing to do. When I read the heroic stories of the People's Liberation Army men, I wanted to be a soldier. When I read articles concerning industrial construction, I wanted to become a locomotive driver. When I read about agriculture, I thought of becoming a peasant in an area where conditions are difficult. In short, I thought by following the Party's instructions I couldn't go wrong. It was with the aim of doing such big things that I went to Panshan.

"When I got to the commune, the Party secretary told me, 'The Hsiangkuoyu Production Brigade is going to lead a river from the other side of the mountain. They welcome people with schooling to take part in the work. You can go there.' I was overjoyed. Two days later, the production brigade leader came to fetch me with a donkey. The first thing I told him was that I wanted to take part in the extension project, to do something big. Scarcely had I finished when a sharp-tongued girl standing behind him (I didn't even notice when she came into the room) put in, 'You are just saying empty words. Do you understand why one wants to do big things?' What manners! I was mad. I would have exploded if I had not been new to the place. She looked as if she wanted to say something else. But the brigade leader winked at her and she stopped short. Before we left, the brigade leader called her outside and reproved her. I only caught the last few words.

" 'Come back immediately after the meeting is over. This task is given to you anyway,' the brigade leader said.

" 'In making iron, you need many people to add coal, but the main thing is to have good ore that can be smelted,' replied the girl.

" 'Good or bad, we'll turn him into fine steel. Well, go to the meeting now. When you come back, we'll get a few people together to talk the matter over.'

"Somehow, I felt they were talking about me.

"Despite all this, my enthusiasm was just as high. I had had my hair close-cropped, and on the way to the village, I splashed mud on my trousers on purpose when we crossed streams and ditches. I thought I would look more like a peasant with these marks.

"As soon as we got to the village, I asked the brigade leader when we were to start the project. He said, 'That still needs some discussion. You can do something else first and acquaint yourself with the farm work!'

" 'Farm work I will do of course,' I thought to myself. 'The sole purpose of my coming here is to work. Will I shirk that?'

"The job assigned to me was an easy one: helping the stockman to remove the haystack. But I sweated so hard that my clothes were soaked through before the morning's work was over, and with the sweat and dust my clothes became very dirty so that I had to change every day. In less than three days, I had no clean clothes left and had to do some washing. At noon, I got a big earthenware basin and began to wash in the courtyard. I was on the point of pouring out the wash water after I finished two vests, when a girl came into the courtyard. Standing by the door, she said gruffly, 'Do you know how far this water was carried here?'

"I was vexed. I looked up and saw it was none other than the sharp-tongued one who rebuked me in the commune office. I frowned and refused to take notice of her. 'Who has hired you to nose into my business?' I thought. 'You think I can't carry water. Well, just wait and see.' I put the vests on a clothesline to dry and went into the room with the rest of the wash.

"Damn it, my fingers were already red and painful after washing just two vests!

"In the afternoon, I asked the villagers working with me where the well was. They said it was at the Old Dragon Pool two *li* away. Before going to bed, I got the water buckets and carrying-pole ready. I went out with them early next morning.

"How beautiful the mountain village looked in the morning! I had never seen such splendid scenery before. The mountains and gullies were a picture of green. Dew-jewelled flowers gave colour to the roadside. Birds flew about overhead, and grasshoppers flitted merrily everywhere. I inhaled the fresh air as I walked on, the buckets dangling and creaking at the ends of the carrying-pole. What a happy thing it was to work in the fields!

"But I was not so happy as I started back with two buckets of water, for I hadn't gone far when I found the load too heavy for me. It caused such pain in my shoulder that I tried to find relief by bending my back or craning my neck. But then my shoulder hurt even more. My legs felt weak and I began to sway back and forth, like people doing the *yangko* folk dance. I could only imagine what a sorry sight I looked. I was about to put down my load and take a rest when someone in front suddenly spoke to me. 'Is it heavy? It's not so easy to get water after all, is it?'

"I raised my head, only to see it was that sharp-tongued girl again. She was just from the village, with two empty buckets on her shoulder-pole and a fancy wash basin under her arm. I gritted my teeth, pretended I was shifting the load to the other shoulder, and walked on.

"The pole had become like a knife cutting into my shoulder. My legs quivered. What a relief I felt when I got to the other side of a gentle slope! I guessed that sharp-tongued girl must have gone down the hill and I could take a rest now, since she wouldn't be able to spot me any more. But when I looked back, I saw her still standing at the top of the hill, watching. How hateful of her! She was obviously looking to see the exhibition I was making of myself. I stiffened and made straight for home. I poured the water into the vat. How I would like to tumble into bed and lie there for a while! But if I didn't turn up for the second buckets, that girl would surely laugh at me. Well, I was not the soft type. I went out again with the buckets.

"It was not a well, just a stone pit. Water dripped at regular intervals from the clefts of the stones, drop by drop, never more, never less. It was rather shallow, with hardly enough water if three people came at one time with their buckets.

"When I arrived for the water, there was that girl sitting calmly by the pit washing clothes. Ignoring her, I stooped to take water. When the buckets were full, I began to leave with the load. 'Take a rest,' she said. I still took no notice of her. 'Irritable, aren't you!' she chided. Before I could explode, she burst into a fit of laughter and laughed so long and hard I thought she was never going to stop. I looked daggers at her. Strange! I suddenly found she was very beautiful, far more charming than any girl I had ever set eyes on before. In her pink and white polka-dot tunic she looked as fresh and lovely as a blossoming lotus against the green background. Her clear, mischievous eyes sparkled like two bright pearls. Her soft but pervading laughter, especially, rang sweeter than an early morning song shaking the dewdrops on the grass in a serene valley. As I looked at her, all my anger against her vanished, and before I knew it I had sat down obediently on the grass. She stopped laughing but went on with the washing. She looked as if she had something to say, so I waited patiently for her to begin. After a while, she nodded and said, 'Yes, you've done quite well. You've got what it takes. Keep on like this, and if you run into difficulties in the future, deal with them the way you did just now. Then nothing can stop you!'

"So, she asked me to sit down to be lectured! I jumped up and left straight away with the buckets. Though I had to grit my teeth all the way, I never turned my head or stopped for breath.

Illustration by Tung Chen-sheng

"When I came to the gate of the house where I stayed, I found she had followed me there. Putting down the fancy basin, she said, 'Hang them up to dry!' It turned out that all the clothes she was washing were mine!

"That night, the brigade leader came to see me, and before leaving, he said, 'Well, Sunflower has picked you out for her team — I'm supposed to assign you. I've promised her. Besides being a team leader, she's a member of the general branch committee of the Youth League. She's smart, straightforward and daring. The young people in her team all like her. You must co-operate with her. You two must learn from each other.'

"But I didn't know such a person, so I asked, 'Who is this Sunflower?'

"'Why, didn't you have a talk at the Old Dragon Pool this morning and settle everything?'

"So, it was she! Who had settled anything with her? But now I was being assigned by the leadership to her team. Although I didn't like the idea, I didn't say so for I knew I ought to obey the leadership.

"Early next morning, Sunflower came to take me onto her team. The majority of the members were young people, so we talked and laughed and were as gay as larks. Sunflower no longer found fault with me as she used to do. On the contrary, she was quite concerned about me. For instance, once I did some hoeing with them. She made a very careful check of my work before we left the field for the day, as thorough as if she were looking for lost treasure and would not go until she found it. In the end she turned to say, 'Not bad for a beginner. But your hoeing posture wasn't very good. Your arms and legs were so stiff one might think you had some kind of paralysis.'

"Another example. In the evening, as I recorded the work-points for the members, she would stand over me, staring at my hand. Once she observed before leaving for home, 'Your handwriting is handsome and clear. It's good to have someone with an education in the team, and you've found the right place for your knowledge. But it won't do to use only your hand and not your head. You must try to discover problems in these figures and help the leader to solve them. Otherwise, you may become a writing machine!'

"You see, that was how she dealt with me, praising and criticizing me at the same time.

"Oddly enough, I would make some progress each time she made such remarks. In hoeing, I began to study how others worked, their stance and movements. As a result, I could not only work with less effort, but I did a better job. In recording work-points, I no longer just put down figures like a machine, but tried to find what was behind them. I discovered that some members had less points because they worked with little enthusiasm. I told the leader about these people so that he could give them some help. The leader was very glad, and I found the work more and more interesting.

"One day, Sunflower took me with her to hoe weeds, the two of us working in the millet fields at the foot of the northern hills. The soil was like cement. Every time I struck with the hoe, it bounced off with a dull clang. And when I pulled on it, it just scudded over the surface. Before long, my arms were numb and painful. I took a closer look at the plot and found there were cracks on it. The millet shoots were thin as hair. A gust of wind could have blown them away.

" 'The soil here is impossible,' I said to Sunflower in spite of myself.

" 'Not at all,' she contradicted. And to prove it, she dug a hole in the ground and showed me the earth inside — dark yellow and really very fertile.

" 'What did you have for breakfast today?' she demanded.

" 'Millet porridge.'

" 'Do you know where the millet came from?'

" 'It's grown in the fields, of course.'

" 'You've got it. All the people in our team depend on these fields for food. We rely on them to yield fodder and feed for our oxen, horses, pigs and chickens. We need them to produce grain to support the state's construction and the people in the cities. But these fields simply refuse to yield anything. The soil is not bad, and we've applied a lot of fertilizer. We don't begrudge our work on them either. Do you know what's lacking?'

"I didn't know. What was lacking, indeed?

"It's w-a-t-e-r that's lacking. Since ancient times, these parts have relied on rain to irrigate the land. If Heaven were angry with us and didn't give rain, we could only watch the shoots thirst to death in the fields. We wouldn't be able even to get the seed back. What could we have for food, feed and fodder? What could we give to support the state and the cities?'

"I nodded in agreement. Swinging the hoe onto her shoulder, she announced, 'The job is done. Let's go home now!'

"From that day on, I became 'water-conscious' and could think of nothing else. I fancied watering the millet even in my dreams.

"A few days later, the brigade formally took up the problem of extending the river. The cadres had a meeting which we Youth Leaguers were invited to attend. After a plan was mapped out, it came to selecting two more people to the committee managing the project. They were to go immediately to a water-conservancy training class in the prefecture. It was specified that they must be ideologically good young people with some education.

"Though I sat by the lamp, I was afraid people might not see me. My heart thumped with nervousness.

"Sunflower was the first to speak. My heart sank as I saw her eyes fixing on me. Turning her head, she said in all seriousness, 'Comrade Young Pine came to the countryside with the determination to do big things. He thought our river project was a big thing and asked to work on it even before he set foot in the village. I said that was only empty talk. I'm sure he must have found my criticism difficult to take. Now I think he no longer indulges in fancies and has become more down-to-earth. Let's elect him as our water-conservancy technician. I believe he will do well on this job.'

"At this unexpected turn in her speech I was filled with joy. I can't find words to describe how I felt then.

"We two went together to the water-conservancy training class run by the Tangshan prefectural government. In those days, she couldn't read and write very fast, and I felt I ought to help her. When we listened to reports and lectures, she had difficulty in taking notes. It made her sweat to listen and jot down notes at the same time. I gave her my notebook to read. She leafed through it and said with a pout, 'It's all spiders. You intentionally made it impossible for people to read!'

"What to do? She wouldn't be able to remember everything by heart. How could she take part in the discussion without notes! So I tried to write distinctly. But then I spent so much time writing, I couldn't keep up with the lecture myself.

"I found a way on the third day. That evening, the students all went out to see a play. I took Sunflower's notebook and stayed behind. When they were gone, I bent over the desk and began copying the notes for her. I didn't even notice when they came back at eleven o'clock. As it was bed-time, I took the work to the reception room and continued. I didn't finish until two o'clock next morning. Don't think I'm boasting, but every stroke, every word was written with great care, and the handwriting was distinct and even. I returned the notebook to Sunflower the next morning. She turned a few pages, nodded and smiled — indication enough of her appreciation. But that was not all. When she spoke, she said, 'I'm not near-sighted. Why did you write the words so big? It's a waste of paper.'

"Despite her criticism, I felt very pleased, because that note-taking was the only way I could give her any help.

"From that day on, I copied notes for her every evening, and my note-copying went on for a whole month without interruption, until we went back to the village.

"Well, talking about going back, I have another episode to tell.

"In the month or so of the training course, both of us were very busy in the free hours. She chatted with one today and joked with another tomorrow. Before many days passed, she had struck up a friendship with everyone. I, on the other hand, would go to the bookshop whenever I had time. Once inside it, I forgot to come out again. So, she was busy with her affairs, and I with mine, and we didn't spend much time together.

"But whenever she saw me buy a new book, she would say, 'Why spend all that money on books? Haven't you enough to read already?'

" 'Books are the treasured sources of knowledge. Without books, how can I become a good technician!' I retorted.

" 'Well, reading books alone won't help with digging the river!'

"There was no point arguing with her, so I just kept silent.

"But as we went home, I suffered. Because our village was still twenty *li* away from the last bus stop, and we had to travel all that distance on foot. She was quite all right, with her light luggage. But I, apart from my heavy bed roll, had an extra bag of books that weighed scores of *jin* to carry. While I sweated profusely under the burden, she laughed and joked all the way at my expense.

" 'Stop cackling. Why don't you help me?' I shouted.

" 'You carry too many burdens. Why don't you get rid of some?'

" 'You mean I should throw away some books?' I asked.

" 'I want you to throw away some burdens in your head.'

"I didn't answer her. We were approaching home anyway.

"We reported to the brigade leader on our study. He said he had already got a new task for us. The course of the new river would be changed. According to the original plan, the river had to make a detour of ten *li* in order to avoid a ravine between the mountain and our fields. To save material and manpower, the brigade leader thought it better to make the river run directly across the ravine. But how this was to be done was entirely up to Sunflower and me.

"We were glad that we were given this task, but were a bit worried at the same time. I asked Sunflower to look for data with me and work out a suggestion. But she didn't want to, saying, 'Digging into books won't get you anywhere.' We began to argue. But neither could convince the other. I went on with my books on engineering, water conservancy and so on. I worked day and night, not even going out of the room. I got very dizzy and my head began to ache, while she just took it easy. On the second day, she rode a bike off to Shanho County, where a fellow-student of the training class lived.

"Three days later, she came back. She laughed heartily when she saw me still buried in books. I refused to take any notice of her.

" 'You're so diligent, scholar. You must have gotten inspiration from a sage!' she ridiculed.

" 'Whether I have or not, I've done my best. I haven't gone and enjoyed the cool on the side,' I retorted.

" 'You think I went for amusement?' she said laughing. 'To tell you the truth, I went to see a water conservancy project in another county. I had heard of it in the training class. I went to have a look for myself.'

" 'Why didn't you tell me?'

" 'I meant to make you put aside your books and go with me. But the brigade leader criticized me, saying I tended to go to one extreme while you went to the other. The right approach was to attach equal importance to theoretical knowledge and practical experience, to combine the two. I thought it sounded right, so I didn't come to pour cold water on you.'

" 'Well then, you've learned their experience, I suppose?'

" 'They've never worked on such projects before either. But they found me some model builders on water conservancy projects and we had a discussion. They told me we could make the water flow across a bridge.'

"That enlightened me. Yes, an aqueduct would do the job. If we built a 'bridge' across the ravine, could not the water flow across it?

"We went to the ravine, surveying the terrain and discussing how the aqueduct was to be built.

" 'What kind of a bridge shall we have?' she asked.

" 'A wooden one,' I replied. But on second thought, I figured wood wasn't suitable. The cost would be too high, and the bridge wouldn't last very long either. 'Maybe we'll have to build a stone one,' I corrected.

" 'But that calls for steel girders and cement. Do we have these things?'

"That put me on the spot again. I felt helpless all the way back.

"All of a sudden, the words 'to combine theoretical knowledge with practical experience' resounded in my ears, and I recalled vaguely I had read something about the Great Wall. It said the arch-shaped openings in the wall were faced entirely with stone and brick, with not a single piece of timber used. It also said that a famous, ancient stone bridge somewhere had a similar structure.

"I told Sunflower what little I knew about it. She was very glad and urged me to find the paragraphs about the wall at once. I plunged into my books as soon as I got home. She also gave a helping hand. Not until midnight did we find the paragraphs. But the description was so brief, we were none the wiser after reading it.

" 'The Great Wall is only eighty *li* away, we'd better go and have a look tomorrow,' said Sunflower.

"The next day we took some food and went to Huang-yai Pass in the Great Wall, had a look around and made a sketch of the archway, then returned to the village and reported our idea to the brigade leader. He thought it was good, and called a meeting to discuss the matter. In the end it was agreed that an aqueduct should be built using the principle of the arch.

"Sunflower and I became more energetic in our work in the subsequent months, digging mud together, coming upon difficulties and overcoming them together with the villagers. And each time we solved a problem, our project went ahead quicker, while at the same time we drew closer to each other.

"That was how we came to know and love each other, and how we got married."

Here the young man stops talking. He leans back comfortably on the bench and looks up at the sky as though engrossed in a happy memory. I, too, fall silent, as if I have just finished a fascinating lyric in one breath.

A crescent moon hangs high in the cloudless sky. It looks like a mouth, smiling sweetly down at the Haiho River, at the happy people there.

But I am not satisfied. "You haven't quite finished yet," I say laughing. "Go on. Your account can hardly qualify as a love story."

He laughs too. "In fact, there's no love story to tell. I can only say that for over a year she had tender feelings for me, and I for her. We were separated only by a thin sheet of window paper — with one poke, the barrier would no longer exist. But neither of us broached the subject. You may not believe it, but we expressed our hopes clearly only a week before we got married.

"After the new river bed was dug, we had a heavy rain, and the water rose sharply. When the torrential flood covered the wooden bridge at the head of the village, all the members of our brigade went out to protect it. For a whole day and night, we drove posts in the storm to strengthen the bridge. Sunflower and I worked together all the time. But then, I could think of nothing but the bridge. We had built it with our own hands. If it collapsed, how could we get to the other side of the river to work the land there? By dawn, only the last post remained to be driven. But I slipped and fell, injuring my leg.

"For the next several days, with me nursing my leg in the house where I stayed, Sunflower came to see me several times a day. She dressed my wound, prepared noodles for me, and told me the brigade news.

"One day after I was better, she came again by dusk and immediately asked me to get up. I obediently did so. She then started to fold and pile up my bedding.

" 'What are you doing?' I asked.

" 'What have you to do with this family that you should live here so long? Move to my house,' she said.

" 'It makes no difference to me. What have I to do with *your* family that I should move to your house?'

" 'Well, Mama says she'd like you for her son-in-law, to take care of her in her old age.'

"And that, you see, is how our relationship was made clear.

"But she did not say any more after I moved into her house.

"Shortly after my leg healed, I got a letter from my mother. She asked me to return to Tientsin to get married. She had chosen a distant cousin at Hsiaochan whom I knew from childhood. My aunt was proposing the match. It only waited for my word, whether I was willing.

"I read the letter to Sunflower without alteration or omission. When I finished, she said as though she hadn't even heard the letter, 'The brigade leader says we mustn't be satisfied just to irrigate the land, now that we have water. We must try and plant rice. It's a high-yield, fine-quality grain. Hsiaochan is a famous rice-producing area. This is a good chance for us to learn how to grow rice. We can begin next year.' Had the message of my mother's letter totally escaped her?

" 'Growing rice is all right,' I said anxiously. 'But how about the marriage!'

" 'That's all right. In fact, that way, both public and private interests will be taken care of. It'll comply with the old folks' wishes and the need to learn how to grow rice as well.'

"Her remark was like an icy bath. Had I been dreaming all the time? I felt very bad and was about to have it out with her when her mother came into the room with some flour she had just ground.

"After supper, I could not contain myself any longer. I called her out to the courtyard and demanded, 'Speak up, Sunflower!'

" 'About what?'

" 'The marriage!'

" 'But haven't I told you what I honestly think about it? If you're impatient, of course, we can go tomorrow. Is that all right?'

"So that's the way it was."

I can't help laughing when he finishes telling all this. So, that is their story, a story of young love fused with the common, socialist cause. Though I have not heard anything on the romantic side of the story, I know that Young Pine would find it very difficult to single out any purely love episode.

Young Pine laughs too, very heartily. "My mother was overjoyed at my bringing her this daughter-in-law, and when we visited my aunt at Hsiaochan she received us with great hospitality and kept us there for seven days. We visited Hsiaochan's expert rice-growers and took full notes on what they said. We came back only yesterday."

"You're spending your honeymoon in the best possible way, I'd say."

"Oh! I forgot." Young Pine suddenly jumps up from the bench and pats the back of his head with his big hand.

"I came here looking for Sunflower! Wait a minute. I must find her at once."

I am perplexed. "Why do you let Sunflower come here all alone?" I ask.

"My mother's so proud of us that she's been taking us around to meet all my father's friends. Just showing off, you know. But we can't afford so much time visiting! Besides, it's so embarrassing. So we found a way out of it. After supper, Sunflower said she was going to the guest house to see an acquaintance, and she left. A little while later I told my mother that Sunflower didn't know the roads and might have trouble finding her way back. So my mother asked me to go at once and fetch her home. I jumped at the chance and slipped out too," he says, laughing mischievously.

Then, quite unexpectedly, he takes me by the shoulder and says seriously, "Old Liang, one point I forgot to tell you. Our Panshan has always been famous for its fruits, such as giant persimmon, small-stone date, autumn pear and fragrant apricot. Since the liberation, many new fruit trees have been planted, and these have begun to bear. Every year, millions of *jin* of fruit have to be sent to the towns and cities on the plain. We have opened tungsten and iron mines too in recent years. All these products, the minerals, plus household necessities and grain, have to be transported by truck, cart and donkey, or carried by men on shoulder-poles. We have more trucks and carts now. But the increase can't keep pace with the growth of production. Transportation has become a big problem — a contradiction difficult to resolve."

Pointing across the river, he continues, "See those boats over there? Sunflower and I happened to pass this way yesterday, and when we saw the boats we thought immediately of the possibility of water transport. When we get back we'll suggest to the leadership to add this new means of transportation. . . ."

I think it is certainly a good idea. "So, you're going to have boats in the mountains?" I query.

He misunderstands me. Shaking his fist, he says with determination, "Why not? We've succeeded in channelling a river from the other side of a mountain so that it gives water to our fields. And we can do more! Our canal is not as large as this river, but it doesn't matter. If we can't use big boats we can use small ones. We can learn to handle boats too. We plan to meet some boat people soon and ask them to teach us. If they agree to take us aboard for a few runs, so much the better. . . . But I've really got to go and find Sunflower. Wait for us here. We'll have a chat together."

With these words, he leaves at a run. I watch his fast retreating figure in the dim moonlight until he is out of sight, and then I hear his voice calling out, "Sunflower, where are you?"

Not long after, I hear the answer. "I'm here, Young Pine. Come at once!" Her voice comes from a boat at the river bank.

I stand up as if instinctively and walk in the direction of the voices. Quite thrilled, I feel like singing aloud.

A summer night on the Haiho River can be very beautiful! And this young couple has given human substance to its beauty.

Tientsin, August 6, 1961

Jade Spring

WITH a letter of introduction from the commune I started my trip to the Winding Hill Village. The commune clerk found a guide for me so that I would not lose my way. This guide, he told me, would meet me at the eastern entrance of the village.

I arrived at the appointed place with my bed roll on my back. The poplars there were so tall that I could not see the tops of them unless I craned my neck. Their broad shiny leaves were rustling in the summer wind. Beneath one of the trees, an old woman and a girl were slowly pushing a stone roller under which the corn turned into minute gold nuggets.

I walked over and asked the old woman if a comrade from the Winding Hill Village had been there.

Before the woman could answer, the girl glanced up and said, "Can't you see we're busy? Wait a minute."

I put my bed roll down on a rock.

"Comrade," said the girl to me, "while you're waiting, why can't you lend us a hand?"

Of course I could. Hadn't I come here to temper myself? So I went over to help them with the roller.

"You go and take a rest in the shade," said the girl to the woman. "The two of us can do the job."

She pushed ahead and, as I followed behind, I saw she was about sixteen or seventeen and of sturdy build. She wore her hair in a braid as thick as a little boy's arm, and it was tied with plastic thread and then a flowered kerchief. She looked back at me now and then as she pushed the stone. A lock of short hair proudly covered her slender eyebrows. Her eyes were unusually bright, and had an innocent and inquiring look. Her small mouth was pursed as if she had something to say but did not. She was agile in movement. She would sweep the ground corn from the stone, then bring in a full pan of kernels. While pushing the roller with one hand, she spread the corn onto the stone with the other as neatly as though each kernel had been laid on by hand. In a short while we had finished grinding a whole bin of the grain.

I kept looking in the direction of the village wondering why my guide hadn't come for me.

The girl swept the corn flour into the dustpan and knocked the dust from her clothes. "We've finished our job. Let's go, comrade," she said.

"But that man hasn't come yet," said I.

"I'll take you there."

The old woman, who was nearby, could not repress a laugh. "She's the one you're looking for. A smart girl, but she likes to play tricks on people!"

So that was it! Everything became clear to me only at this moment!

Casually, the girl reached up to a tree branch on tiptoe and took down a book that was there. She picked a leaf from the branch and inserted it to mark a page of the book, then tucked it under her arm.

"Let's start now. Why waste time!" She blinked once, then continued, "This auntie is an old poor peasant, a dependent of a martyr. The Youth League members of our production brigade have agreed that whoever of us goes to the commune on an errand should pay her a visit and help her with some chore. I've only finished half the work and it isn't very good just to leave it and go with you. Don't you think so?"

"But you should have told me," I said.

She smiled. "Haven't you come for practice in physical labour? That was a test I was giving you."

2

We proceeded along a path on a slope. Except for the path the whole area was green — dark green, with a few flowers here and there, like white and yellow lanterns gladdening the eye. Birds and insects were chirping, flying or leaping about in the bushes and among the flowers, making a lively scene all round.

The girl offered to take a turn carrying my bed roll and walked ahead over the rugged path as easily as on a well-paved road. As I followed behind, I discovered that the book she had was a novel.

"Do you like to read novels?" I asked.

She shook her head. "I like books on botany best. But our old brigade leader insists we read novels. Says it's compulsory reading!" She giggled as she continued, "Of course, that's not why I'm reading one, but my work requires it."

"You should read more works on literature and art," I suggested.

Shaking her head, she said, "Our brigade leader says reading a novel should not be made a pastime or a fashion. He says I must learn to take up the novel as a weapon in the class struggle of our countryside."

Curt, straightforward and vigorous, she was a girl with whom you could never get angry. You couldn't help liking her!

"What's your name?" I asked.

"Guess," she said.

I couldn't.

"Well, I'll tell you. My name is Tsui Chuan."

The name was new and sounded strange to me. So she explained, "Tsui means green like jade, and Chuan means mountain stream, so I'm called Jade Spring. To the north of our village is a stony ditch, and a stream flows from a cleft in the rock. It flows in summer and winter, in spring and fall, without stopping. Our brigade leader says it doesn't dry up because its source is deep and its course long. In a few years the trees planted on its banks will have grown tall and the sun will throw their shadows on it, mirroring an exquisite jade green. . . ."

"Ah! You're a poetess!" I exclaimed.

She only smiled and then said thoughtfully, "It's a joy to look at. Though small, it seems to have inexhaustible energy, and is never erratic, never failing."

Was she writing a poem, or just thinking? I was at a loss.

She suddenly stopped and asked me, "Say, comrade, is your Peking beautiful?"

"Of course, it is."

"How?"

"I can't describe it in a few words," said I. "It's our capital, the country's political and cultural centre. There you can see the most splendid things. . . ."

"Can't you be more specific."

"Well, as for ancient buildings, there are the Summer Palace, the Imperial Palaces, the Temple of Heaven and the Peihai Park. Then there are the new buildings which have appeared since liberation, such as the Great Hall of the People, the Peking Railway Station, the Cultural Palace of Nationalities, the National Agricultural Exhibition Centre, and many others. They all add to the beauty of Peking. . . ."

She listened attentively and became animated with the excitement of it. Abruptly, she stopped me. "Are the people living in Peking all happy?" she asked.

"Of course."

"I don't think so." And she shook her head.

I was surprised at her remark but remembered I must be on guard in case she was teasing me again. But this time she seemed to be serious.

"I think a lot of Peking — really!" said she.

"Have you been there?" I asked.

Smiling and still thoughtful, she replied, "I think I must have been there. Peking has always been in my heart. I've come to the conclusion that Peking must be as lovely as our Winding Hill Village. . . ."

I smiled at the remark.

She was keen enough to feel my reaction, and said seriously, "Don't laugh. That's how I feel. Tell me, does the beauty of Peking drop from the sky?" Then, walking ahead a few steps, she continued, "Once I really went to Peking. I was standing before the Tienanmen Gate having my photograph taken. That photographer was very particular; he wanted me to smile. So I did, but my smile turned into laughter which woke up my mother. She gave me a little slap. . . ."

I burst out laughing.

She became thoughtful again. "Now, I won't go there even if someone presents me with the train ticket!"

"Why?" I wondered. "Don't you dream of going there?"

"I dream of going, but I won't go."

"What makes you say that?"

"If Chairman Mao should ask me, 'Have you built up your village?' What could I say? I can't go to Peking empty-handed."

Now I saw something of this girl's depth of vision.

Before I knew it we had entered the pretty settlement known as the Winding Hill Village.

She put my bed roll on the ground and wiped the sweat from her face. "Here you are. When you've put your things down where you're going to stay, come to our house for a while." She ran off towards the South Street, her big braid swinging.

3

I lodged on the North Street.

My hosts were an old couple — the production brigade leader, who was sixty-four and whom Jade Spring constantly mentioned, and his wife. Their children were all away. He was frank, straightforward and capable, and she was warm-hearted. Once acquainted, we quickly became like members of one family.

After dinner the brigade leader went out on an errand while his wife finished washing the dishes and chopsticks. Picking up a small stool, she said to me, "It's cooler out in the street. Let's go there. We have a habit of going out onto the street after dinner when the weather gets warm — the whole family goes. Recently some old folks have invited a story-teller, so a lot of people turn out. The Party branch thinks it isn't good to tell only old stories and has arranged for a new story to be told this evening. Let's go and listen to the new story and see if it is interesting."

When we reached the street, we saw commune members, men and women, coming out from their houses carrying fans, walking towards a big walnut tree at the bridge head. A crowd had already gathered under a dim oil lamp. Some were talking and laughing loudly, some were soothing the children in their arms.

The hubbub died down when a man swaggered into the crowd. I could not see his face as the moon was at his back. I only saw someone hand him a stool to sit down. Taking a sip of tea, puffing on his pipe, and with a cough, he began, "Folks, today we'll tell the story of Tou Erh-tun stealing the emperor's horse. . . ."

My hostess, the brigade leader's wife, squeezed herself into the crowd, looked around and asked, "Mister, isn't it true a new story will be told this evening?"

Someone echoed, "That's right. The brigade leader said last night that from now on there's to be no more telling of trash."

Another one earnestly requested, "Please tell a new story, one that will open our eyes."

The story-teller shook his head and looked at the man who had made the request. "I'm sorry, folks," he said slowly. "I can't tell new stories. If you must hear a new one, please ask someone else who is more competent."

A few others got impatient. "Never mind," they said. "Let's hear any story you have to tell."

"Anything will do. It's for amusement," some others added.

At this moment someone called from the sidelines, "Comrades Commune Members, if you want to listen to a new story, please come over here."

I looked and saw a group of people sitting under a big walnut tree on which hung a brilliant lamp. The man who was calling was no other than the old brigade leader.

"Look. Here comes a competitor," said my hostess, nudging me. "It must be a new story. No mistake. Let's go over there."

And she took me to where the light was.

The audience was almost all young people and village cadres. They surrounded the story-teller — the girl who had accompanied me to this village, Jade Spring!

She was sitting on a small stool under the light with a book on her knee, *The Story of Liu Hu-lan*, which she had borrowed from the commune library that morning. She seemed a little nervous, turning the pages of the book or moving the stool with unsteady hand.

The brigade leader, a short-stemmed pipe in his mouth, and smiling, whispered something to Jade Spring.

The Youth League secretary brought a flowered porcelain teapot and a cup, poured tea into the cup, placed it before her and said, "Take a sip and get going. Give it a lot of pep!"

The woman leader also came. She turned the lamp up to make it brighter. "Start right now, Jade Spring. Our story-telling will go on even if there's only one person in the audience. Get lamp oil from my house if there isn't enough."

Jade Spring looked up and around at the people. Her eyes began to sparkle and she commenced, "Comrades Commune Members, I've just borrowed this book. I haven't the story well in mind, but I'll try. I've selected a chapter titled "Liu Hu-lan Died a Martyr."

"Good!"

"Fine!"

The audience clapped in approval.

Jade Spring's story attracted more and more people from the other side. All were moved and inspired by Liu Hu-lan's revolutionary deeds and heroic sacrifice. They sat quietly throughout the telling of the story, and were reluctant to leave even when it was over.

I walked back with the brigade leader under a waning moon and we talked all the way. He told me about Jade Spring.

The girl was her mother's pet. For generations the poor people of the Winding Hill Village could not read or write, and girls had still less chance to learn than boys. Schools were set up only after liberation. Jade Spring was among the first group of girl students. The villagers all liked her and the cadres thought highly of her. When she was a second-grade pupil in the primary school, the old brigade leader set up the first mutual-aid team and asked her to be a spare-time work-point recorder. However, she could not work out the total figures in all the ten books, so the brigade leader taught her arithmetic by counting little stones and drawing lines, while they sat under the big walnut tree. Finally she was able to work out the total figures. That year she did good work as a work-point recorder, and in school she was at the head of the class in arithmetic. When she reached the higher primary grades, the brigade leader, who had taken the lead in organizing the agricultural co-operative, asked her to serve as spare-time clerk. But she could not write more than three lines of a report. Again it was the brigade leader who coached her, dictating and correcting sentence by sentence. She wrote a lot of reports that year, and when the examination was given on composition, she rated first in her class in that subject too. When she entered middle school, the village formed a people's commune, and she served as its spare-time publicity worker. Whenever a meeting, big or small, was held, the brigade leader would ask her to come as soon as she finished her lessons. By hard work and with good coaching she became an all-round student in school.

Though she grew capable through practical struggle, her mother regarded all her good points as "inborn talent." She had great expectations of her, saying Jade Spring would be "somebody" one day. When the girl finished junior middle school, her mother considered her remaining in the village a problem and wanted her to leave home and go out into the wide world.

"You have no room for me at home?" Jade Spring asked her mother.

"It isn't because Mother wants to throw you out. It's because the little gully here is too small for you."

The mother tried a thousand and one ways to make her daughter soar to the skies, but the daughter had only one way — she wouldn't budge. For a whole year the mother had failed in every attempt. Now she had a bright idea. An uncle of Jade Spring's worked in a drug store in Peking. He had everything he wanted in life except children. He liked Jade Spring very much for her good character and ability and wished to adopt her. Some days ago Jade Spring's mother had received a letter from him suggesting that the girl go to Peking to live and study in a higher school, or work there. Jade Spring refused the offer and was having an argument with her mother.

"Jade Spring's mother is muddle-headed," the brigade leader remarked at this point in the story. "She's forgotten how we old poor peasants suffered in the past. She insists that her daughter's gifted and that she won't be able to shine in the countryside. She doesn't understand that her daughter has deep roots here. Jade Spring has a head full of knowledge that comes only from plenty of tempering in the collective. For more than a year she's given no small service to the village. She works like any grown-up, and can write, draw and talk equally well. The four blackboard bulletins are all edited and written by her, and they're changed every three days. The speaker system seems to have been set up specially for her; her voice is like music. Her microphone and blackboard bulletins spread stories of good people and their good deeds. While we are building up the countryside, young people like her are very much needed. What can she do if she doesn't answer the need of the country and of the collective, if she leaves physical labour and the struggle here? We're trying now to convince her mother and win her over to our view. The road before Jade Spring is broad and smooth. Her taking it depends on whether she listens to the Party or not. Of course, she's still young and acts like a child in many ways. So we must give her constant advice and guidance; we must give more thought to her."

The brigade leader's story of Jade Spring moved me like lyric poetry.

4

Jade Spring had always appeared like a happy little bird singing and flitting about. But one day before lunch when I was in the courtyard of the house where I stayed, I saw her for the first time sitting quietly on a stool, patching a white jacket for the brigade leader. As she quietly plied her needle, she appeared quite gentle and elegant.

On seeing me, she hastily made a few more stitches, broke off the thread and sprang up to complain of me, "Where have you been? I've been looking for you the whole morning. I have a request to make of you."

We went into the room and she took from her pocket a sheet of paper and an envelope, laid the paper on the table, asked me to sit down, then took a pen and thrust it into my hand.

"Will you write a letter for me?" she said very seriously.

I thought she was fooling me again and stood up to go.

"Don't kid me! To think of an educated person like you asking me to write a letter for you!" I told her plainly.

Agitated, she urged me again, "I'm serious. Take down what I tell you and don't ask questions. Understand?"

Seeing her earnestness I sat down.

She began to dictate: " 'Dear Sister-in-law. For your honourable attention.' Now write!"

I wrote down these words.

" 'Is your honourable health fine?' "

I couldn't help laughing.

"What's so funny? That person just likes to play with words, but his style is neither literary nor vernacular. Now go on. 'Concerning our niece's schooling and work, I have consulted my wife many times. This matter has to do with her future; it is better to give it further consideration. . . .' "

I followed her dictation.

Both hands gripping the table edge, her eyes shining, she gazed out of the window at the hills and trees beyond, stopped a moment and continued, " 'The countryside is now carrying on socialist construction. This cause has the greatest bearing on the happiness of future generations. It is a cause our forefathers never dreamed of. It is most dignified, most glorious for young people living in this age to sweat a little for this cause.' "

As her feeling rose, her face became stern. She clenched both fists as she continued:

" 'As you, Sister-in-law, said, our niece is a smart girl. But what has made her smart is the physical labour, life and struggle in the countryside, and it is in the countryside that she can prove her worth and where she has a great future . . .' "

With a shake of her head she threw back the lock of hair that was bothering her. "Please write," she reminded me solemnly. " 'Take that stream to the north of the village. It is fed from the surrounding hills and so becomes a beautiful and useful rivulet, flowing ceaselessly. If you moved it to another place, it would dry up. If a young person leaves the road pointed out by the Party, abandons the collective and the revolution, that young person will lose all vitality. NO, I WON'T DO IT!' "

I was startled by her sudden outburst.

Stopping for a minute and biting her lips, she went on, "Say, don't write that last sentence. Delete it if you have already. Now continue: 'Don't look down upon the countryside. Without rural construction, how can you have beautiful cities?'

"Come on, hurry!" She put a finger at the place on the paper. "Here, continue from this line: 'In time the countryside will be as beautiful as the cities. Haven't we begun to plant trees to turn the barren hills into vast green slopes and build reservoirs and power stations? With fruit trees, water and power, and with all kinds of power-driven machines, the mountain area will prosper. Whoever still belittles the countryside is mixed up in his thinking.' Wait a minute. Let me think. Shall I add this?" She knit her brows, then her nod showed her decision. "Yes, I will! Now continue: 'We should respect our niece's wish to remain in the countryside and become an educated peasant of the new generation and a red successor in building the new socialist countryside.' "

I finished writing the letter as she directed. She took it, read it over and asked me to correct a few places, then write the name "Chen Fu-teh" at the end. I didn't understand what all this meant, but she would not answer my questions. Finally she put the letter into an envelope and ran out in high spirits.

I followed her to the gate and saw her speaking to my hostess. I could not hear what she was saying but I saw my hostess laughing heartily as she took the letter, patted her clothes and walked off.

About half an hour later Jade Spring's mother came into the courtyard and asked, "Is Comrade Liang in?"

I went out to meet her.

"I've come to ask you to read a letter for me," said the woman. "It's from my brother-in-law in Peking. It must have been written in a hurry. I can't make it out."

I was stumped when I saw the letter. It was the one I had just written for Jade Spring!

"Please read it to me. What does it say?" the woman asked.

When I began, I stuttered as if I was reading a foreign language. As I went on things became clear to me.

Jade Spring's mother stood stupefied and said nothing when I finished reading.

My hostess came over and asked her, "Well, what does the letter say? Will Comrade Liang read it again — to me?"

"Please don't," said the mother. "It's the same as Jade Spring, the brigade leader and others say. I don't need him lecturing me. Don't I know my own daughter?"

"No, you don't, that's it," said my hostess. "Do you know she's made up her mind to stay in the countryside? And you insist that she leave here."

The mother sighed. "If everyone says so, perhaps she's right. Let her decide. I give up!"

Just then Jade Spring rushed in, threw her arms round her mother's neck and, laughing, cried out, "Mother, you've consented. You must keep your word!"

My hostess and I laughed till we were out of breath. Then, in the midst of it, the brigade leader walked in. His tanned, dark face was very grave. He looked at us and turned to Jade Spring.

"This is a serious matter," he said. "Why should you try to settle it by childish pranks? When you choose your road of life, it should be open, frank and above-board. You can never settle a question by using tricks. You'll only show yourself in the wrong. With sound reasoning you can always convince others. Even if you yourself can't argue well, you can depend on the people around you."

Jade Spring was stunned for a moment. Then, realizing she was wrong in forging the letter, she bowed her head.

Turning to the mother, the brigade leader said, "Please sit down, sister. Let's have a chat. What was written in the letter did not come from your brother-in-law but sprang from your daughter's heart. We oldsters should know how to love our children and how to guide them onto the right path. Can't you calm down and think it over? Sit down."

Embarrassed, she sat on the edge of the *kang*. "Comrade Liang, will you read the letter again?" she managed to stammer.

5

As the crescent moon rose, the village was bathed in its silver light. The cooling wind wafted the fragrance of swaying wistaria.

From the speaker came the voice of Jade Spring, "Comrades Commune Members. . . ." The voice sounded firmer, more forceful and attractive than ever before. The folks who were sitting in their courtyards or in the street cooling themselves began immediately to listen.

"The brigade committee says that beginning tomorrow morning we shall plant trees by the stream. This is the start of our fight to transform the barren hills. We will not only make grain grow out from between rocks, but also timber, fruit, and other good things. Today we plant seedlings. Five years from now we'll have the fruits. We'll turn the hills and dales into granaries and orchards. . . ."

Sitting next to the brigade leader, I listened attentively. I seemed to see her excited, smiling face.

That evening we turned in earlier than usual, as we had to get up the next morning at daybreak to plant the trees. I was just dropping off when I was awakened by knocks at the window, and a low voice calling: "Get up, Comrade Liang. Get up."

"Is it Jade Spring?" I asked.

"Not so loud. Come outside and I'll tell you something."

I dressed hurriedly and went out, wondering what was up.

Standing near the window with a flashlight in her hand, the girl appeared to be in an excited but happy mood. She pulled me by the sleeve out to the street and then said, "It's wonderful! I just telephoned the commune and was told the apple saplings had arrived. Let's go and get them."

I looked at the moon setting beyond the hills.

At once she guessed what I was thinking. "Afraid of the dark?" asked she. "I'll lead the way. With a flashlight I assure you we won't fall into a ditch. The apple saplings were dug out three days ago. The earlier we plant them the more of them will grow. I won't feel at ease until the saplings are in our hands."

Winding our way over the hill path we reached the commune. The clerk had already divided out the saplings and bundled up our share. Jade Spring hurriedly picked them up and walked off, forgetting to say "thanks."

The moon had set. Nothing could be seen in the gully. The peak and woods were all in darkness.

I suggested we find a stick so that the two of us could carry the bundle.

"No need," she said. "We'll take turns carrying it."

After a while I walked up. "Now, it's my turn," I told her.

"In a while," she said without turning her head.

"Now give it to me." I caught her up.

"Just a minute." She walked faster.

So I chased after her till we reached the edge of the village. I was displeased and asked her why she had led me on that merry chase without even letting me help her carry the bundle.

"To tell you the truth," she said, "I've never in all my life been out in the dark. Of course I was afraid. But after tonight's trip, I see it's the same, day or night — nothing to be afraid of. I wouldn't have asked you to come with me if I had known this before."

So, she just wanted company!

When we were in the village she put down the saplings, took a deep breath, wiped off her sweat, looked up at the stars and said, "Now, go back to sleep. It's late."

"Didn't you say you wanted to plant them right away?"

"A few hours' difference doesn't matter. Better get some sleep. We have a lot of work to do tomorrow. I'll get a nap too."

And, shouldering the saplings, she was off.

At dawn the brigade leader came to wake me up. Each carrying a hoe, we went out of the village and walked towards the North Gully.

It was an early June morning. A light fog shrouded the peak, floated over the tree tops and the rivulet and lingered on the granite steps of the embankment. The rugged gully seemed to have softened. Vapour rose from the stream, whose gurgle I could hear from a distance. On its bank was someone bending down one moment and standing up at another, or busily moving about.

The brigade leader nudged me and whispered, "See! Jade Spring got up even earlier. A wise girl, and she's got her wish."

She saw us, and ran and jumped over the stream to meet us. She had sweat on her forehead, and her trouser-legs were wet and plastered with dewy grass. In a muddy hand was a pick.

"Look, apple trees!" she exclaimed joyfully, waving her hand.

"What apple trees?" asked the brigade leader who did not catch what she had said.

"There!" she pointed them out to him.

Ah, a row of apple saplings had been planted by the stream. Wet soil covered their roots, while the morning sun tinged the young branches with colour.

The brigade leader strode over to the saplings. Blinking he counted, "One, two, three, four, five . . . thirty! When did you plant them? You must have stayed up all night."

The girl smiled but avoided answering the question.

"Brigade leader," she said, "I followed the directions you gave us yesterday and marked off the areas for timber and orchard so that the commune members can do the planting at once. Will you see if I have marked them off correctly?"

Taking a folded paper from her pocket and spreading it on the grass, she added, "I've also sketched the distribution of different kinds of trees according to the brigade committee's plan."

The brigade leader and I got down to look at the sketch with her. It showed the distribution of fruit trees in red and green, with a blue stream running through. At this moment the sun threw its light on the picture, as if giving it life — the leaves turning green, the trees blossoming, the stream flowing and reflecting all.

"Brigade leader," said Jade Spring, "let's just stay here and watch the saplings grow. We'll put up sheds."

"I can do that. Why should you stay out in the wilds?"

Illustration by Tung Chen-sheng

"I want to watch the saplings put down roots, put forth young tender leaves and rich blossoms, bear fruit made rosy by the sun. Mother agrees to my remaining in the village for the rest of my life. I want to do my work as I should."

The picture of a green countryside before me and the voice of the girl ringing in my ears, I was deeply stirred. I suddenly remembered the first time I met her when she asked me a question.

"Jade Spring," I said, "that day when I said Peking was beautiful, you replied that it must be as beautiful as the Winding Hill Village. When I answered you that people living in Peking were all happy, you didn't agree with me. I wondered why you thought that way. Now I understand."

A little insect crawled onto the paper. Flipping it off, she said thoughtfully, "You should have known. Peking is beautiful because its builders are fine people. By dint of hard work people can make a place that's not so beautiful into a magnificent one. If you have no socialist consciousness, no will to devote your whole life to socialism, but only wait for other people to build Peking into a lovely place and then go there to enjoy what others have built with their labour without lifting a finger yourself, you will never be happy."

Jade Spring, you are a smart girl indeed! You are a happy girl!

Peking, December 27, 1964

彩　霞

浩　然　著

董辰生、陈玉先插图

*

外文出版社出版（北京）
1974年（34开）第一版
编号：（英）10050—772
00130（精）
00100（平）
10—E—1317